Praise for Rachel Lee

"Conard County is a wonderful place to visit."
—*New York Times* bestselling author
Heather Graham Pozzessere

"Rachel Lee's Conard County is a place where
every romance reader's dreams come true
in the most wonderful of ways."
—Melinda Helfer, *Romantic Times BOOKreviews*

"A suspenseful, edge-of-the-seat read."
—*Publishers Weekly* on *Caught*

Praise for Catherine Mann

"Catherine Mann's picture should be in the dictionary
next to 'superb.' Military romance fans rejoice!"
—*New York Times* bestseller Suzanne Brockmann

"Catherine Mann delivers a powerful,
passionate read not to be missed!"
—*New York Times* bestseller Lori Foster

"Mann joins Suzanne Brockmann and
Merline Lovelace in my ranks of must-read
(and collect) authors."
—*NoveList*

RACHEL LEE

was hooked on writing by the age of twelve, and practiced her craft as she moved from place to place all over the United States. She now resides in Florida and has the joy of writing full-time.

Her bestselling *Conard County* miniseries has won the hearts of readers worldwide, and it's no wonder, given her own approach to life and love. As she says, "Life is the biggest romantic adventure of all—and if you're open and aware, the most marvelous things are just waiting to be discovered."

CATHERINE MANN

RITA® Award winner Catherine Mann blasted onto the scene five years ago and already has over twenty books on the shelves in multiple languages. Also a Bookseller's Best winner and a five-time RITA® Award finalist, she has spent the past nineteen years following her military flyboy husband around the country with their four children in tow, currently landing in the Florida panhandle. Catherine enjoys hearing from readers and chatting on her Web site message board—thanks to the wonders of wireless Internet, which allows her to cyber-network with her laptop by the ocean! For more information, visit her Web site at www.catherinemann.com.

RACHEL LEE
AND
CATHERINE MANN

Holiday Heroes

Silhouette®

Romantic

SUSPENSE

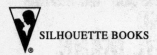

SILHOUETTE BOOKS

ISBN-13: 978-0-373-27557-1
ISBN-10:   0-373-27557-9

HOLIDAY HEROES

Copyright © 2007 by Harlequin Books S.A.

The publisher acknowledges the copyright holder of the individual
works as follows:

A SOLDIER FOR ALL SEASONS
Copyright © 2007 by Susan Civil-Brown and Cristian Brown

CHRISTMAS AT HIS COMMAND
Copyright © 2007 by Catherine Mann

Visit Silhouette Books at www.eHarlequin.com

Printed in U.S.A.

CONTENTS

A SOLDIER FOR ALL SEASONS
Rachel Lee

To peace, which can only be achieved through love

Chapter 1

Jon Erikson wandered into Conard City, Wyoming, like a man lost in the midst of a wild blizzard. Only he wasn't lost, he had grown up here. But it had been so long, and he'd been so far away, that he felt more lost than he had since his first days in Afghanistan.

He found Mahoney's Bar where it had always been. The thought of bellying up to the bar and ordering a beer had been whirling in his dreams for a long time now. Stomping the snow off his boots, he walked inside.

Nothing had changed, except some of the faces. They all turned to look at him, but none seemed to recognize him. Why should they? He hadn't been back here in a long, long time.

Only Mahoney gave him a second glance, as he drew a draft beer for him and put it in front of him. "I know you?" Mahoney asked finally.

Jon wasn't sure he wanted to answer, but finally he said, "I lived here a long time ago."

Mahoney nodded. "Must've been a kid. You look like you've put in a lot of tough miles."

Jon gave him a nod, then lifted the frothy beer to his mouth.

Mahoney didn't press him any further, apparently figuring it was none of his business. Jon was grateful. He wanted, needed, to be left alone for a while.

The bar was too warm. He wasn't used to central heating any longer. Worse, it seemed to be closing in on him. And the beer…it didn't taste as good as he remembered.

He told himself to cool it, that things were just fine, but he honestly couldn't remember the last time he hadn't felt wired and wasn't sure he knew how to unwind.

So drink your beer and just wait.

The tension would have to let go, sooner or later. There wasn't a threat within thousands of miles. But while his brain knew that, the rest of him seemed unable to accept it. He downed the beer and ordered another one, standing with his foot on the rail, rather than sitting on one of the stools.

"Hey," said a quiet female voice.

Every muscle in his body tensed, and he automatically reached for the weapon that wasn't there.

"Relax," she said. "I just thought I recognized you."

He turned slowly and looked at a pretty dark-haired young woman, maybe twenty-five or so, dressed in a State Park Ranger's uniform with an unzipped green parka over it.

"Aren't you Jon Erikson?" she asked.

He nodded slowly, uneasy at being recognized. That, too, had been trained into him.

Her smile started at her blue eyes, then traveled down to pink lips. "I thought so. You were three years ahead of me in school, so you probably never noticed me. I had a crush on you, though."

He should know how to respond to that. Words should come automatically. Something light, something about how could he possibly have overlooked her, kid or not. Some distant part of his brain remembered how to be sociable, but such things had been burned out of him a while back.

"I'm Melinda Hawthorne," she said, sticking out her hand. "State Park Ranger in these woods."

He shook her hand automatically, then abruptly became acutely aware of the warmth of her skin. It wasn't soft skin; clearly she worked hard with her hands. But it was warm, and human, and it wasn't threatening.

"You look like you could use something to eat,"

she said. "We can eat a sandwich here, or go over to the City Diner and have a bigger bite."

"You asking?"

"I'm buying," she said with a laugh. "It's not often I meet someone from that far back who hasn't been around ever since. I want to hear about the big world."

"Can't tell you much. I've spent most of my time in…" He trailed off. He didn't want to talk about that.

"I know," she said, taking his arm. "Come on, let's go to Maude's. You need one of her steak sandwiches and fries."

Now that *did* sound good. He was so damn sick of MREs—meals ready to eat? What a joke—and goat cheese. "Fine, but *I'm* buying," he said.

She shook her head. "I always go Dutch. Unless I buy."

"Dutch it is."

What the hell was going on? A few minutes ago he'd been living in his isolated world with his miserable self, and all of a sudden he'd been yanked out of it by a girl he couldn't even remember.

But she remembered him. And somehow, surprisingly, that made him feel good. As if somehow some part of him *hadn't* died over there.

Closing up their jackets and pulling up their hoods, they stepped out into the blowing snow. "This is global warming," she said, raising her voice to be heard over the wind.

"Yeah, that makes sense."

"I'm not kidding. We never used to get so much snow or so many blizzards. But I don't want to argue about it."

Maude's wasn't very far, although tonight it was fairly deserted. Maude herself was the only one on duty, and in her usual welcoming way she stomped over to the table, slapped the menus down and said, "Coffee's fresh, kitchen's pretty much closed 'cause of the storm, but I can make you steak sandwiches and fries."

Melinda answered with a smile. "That's exactly what we came for, Maude."

Maude grunted, then looked more closely at Jon. "Aren't you the Erikson kid? Old Lars's son?"

Jon nodded.

Maude put her hands on her hips and frowned at him. "Boy, you can't be much over thirty. Whatever you're doing with your life ain't healthy for you."

Then she turned and stomped away, leaving Melinda and Jon to look at one another across a Formica tabletop. Jon had chosen the seat with his back to the wall so he could see the entire room. But now, as he finally met Melinda's eyes again, he saw something dark there, something that belied her outward friendliness and easy smiles.

And somehow that darkness called to him. At once he looked away, disturbed.

"So," she said, "you left town a couple of days after graduation. Everyone said you'd enlisted."

He nodded, reluctantly looking at her again.

"Marines, if I remember right."

"Yes."

She frowned faintly. "Given what the Marines have been doing for the last few years, I guess you haven't been playing golf."

"Not exactly." He felt his nerves tightening again, winding up as if a grenade were about to land in his lap.

"Sorry," she said, and let it go. As if she understood that he still felt like a combination of hunted animal and predator.

Maude brought two mugs of coffee and plunked them down on the table with her usual lack of grace. "Five minutes on them sandwiches," she said and stalked away. Maude always seemed angry with the world, and somehow that thread back to his childhood days made his surroundings feel more real to Jon. The ever-present prickle at the base of his skull eased.

"I love Maude," Melinda said. "No matter what goes on in the world, she's always the same. She'll always grumble when she serves the same menu year in and out. Nobody in the world makes fat taste as good."

Jon felt a smile tug at the corners of his mouth. It felt good. "My arteries are hardening already."

"Every month I come into town from my place in the park, and the first thing I do is stoke up on Maude's food. Well, maybe the second thing. I always get a draft at Mahoney's, too." She paused for a moment. "How long are you in town for?"

"I'm not sure." He didn't have to ship out for another three weeks, but whether he wanted to spend all that time here was something he hadn't really decided, even though he had no idea where else he would go, except maybe to visit some buddies who'd come home wounded.

"Well, if you're still here in two weeks, why don't you come with me to the Tates' for Christmas dinner. You remember the Tates."

"How could anyone not? Is he still sheriff?"

"Absolutely. Do you think anyone would be crazy enough to run against Nate Tate?"

His faint smile broadened. "Probably not."

"He's a good guy." Something passed like a shadow across her face, then vanished before he was even certain he'd seen it.

Maude brought their steak sandwiches, slapped the hot plates on the table and shook her head again. "Boy, you look like you been hung out to dry."

Then, before he could think of an answer, she vanished back into her kitchen.

"You really *don't* look so good," Melinda said. "Like you need to be fed, and you need some rest. Where are you staying?"

"The La-Z-Rest."

"Stupid question," she said with a little laugh. "Where else could anyone stay here? I'm staying there, too, even though ordinarily I'd go back tonight. You'd be amazed how much trouble people can get themselves into by going into the mountains in winter."

"No, I wouldn't be surprised."

She looked at him straight on, then nodded. "No, I suppose you wouldn't."

The blizzard was blowing even harder by the time they stepped out of Maude's.

"My car's just over there," Melinda said, pointing to a heap of snow.

"Are you sure we can find it?"

She laughed. "We'd better, or it's going to be a cold walk."

He helped her brush the snow off a park service four-wheel-drive truck, one of the big ones, and painted that icky green that park services seemed to like. The tires were studded, so they stuck to the road pretty well as she drove through the deepening drifts in the streets.

At the motel, she bade him good-night as soon as they were out of the car.

He stood in the blowing snow, hardly feeling the cold, watching her disappear into a room four doors down from his. Then he entered his own room and closed the door.

At once he felt as if he were in a tomb. Too quiet. Too warm. Not even a draft under the door.

He turned off the heater under the window at once

and opened the window a crack. Cold air snaked into the room, transforming it, and the keening of the wind could be heard.

Only then did he flop into the bed and slip into what he hoped would be a dreamless sleep.

Chapter 2

Melinda had trouble sleeping. Something about Jon Erikson had gotten under her skin. The contrast between the high schooler she remembered and the man he had become was so stark as to be upsetting. She couldn't imagine what he had endured.

Not that she was the same person she had been, either. Innocence had been stripped from her at sixteen by a crazy man. Innocence and her sense of security. To this day, she really only felt safe in the woods and mountains, where her skills could protect her from nearly everything.

Other people might be threats. In the park she only needed to see them when necessary, and there was always a gun on her hip and a shotgun in her truck. Not to mention all the martial arts she'd studied.

Out there it was almost impossible for anyone to approach her without warning. Out there, people were few and far between, and that was the way she liked it.

But running into Jon Erikson today had reminded her of how much she had changed since he left. Just as he had changed almost beyond recognition.

The girlish crush she'd had back then was so far away she couldn't believe she had ever felt it. And the man she had met this evening was not someone a woman could have a crush on. Hardness filled him. Inside him, she had sensed emotional granite. Maybe the Marines did that to a person. Maybe that was the only way to survive.

She knew something about survival, but not that kind, not to that degree.

Finally, tired of tossing in a bed that was not her own, she got up and went to the window, pulling the curtain back to look out at the blizzard. Thank goodness she didn't have any registered hikers or skiers in the park right now. If there were any, she would be out in this hunting them down.

The snow was so thick and whipped so wildly in the light from the motel that she couldn't even see all the way across the parking lot.

Global warming. Everyone thought the weather would just get hotter. If she were to make a bet on it, she would bet on the next ice age. Of course, no one could say for certain, but paleoclimatology suggested that when the earth warmed just a few degrees, it went quickly into an ice age.

Which would explain the kind of weather they'd been having here for the last ten years or so.

She smiled at herself. Being a park ranger had turned her into a rabid environmentalist. She watched the trees grow higher up the mountainsides year to year as the carbon dioxide level rose in the atmosphere, just as she watched the winters get worse. And try as she might, she still had to use a gas-powered vehicle and a gas-powered generator at times.

No way around it.

But the snow was pretty, whirling like dervishes out there, turning the night bright with its reflection of the light. It brought back childhood memories of waking up in the morning to a suddenly hushed world, realizing that the first snow had fallen. Memories of rare snow days that fell like a gift from the heavens, giving her the opportunity to disappear into fresh snow, slide down the hill behind the house, make snowmen…. It had been so magical then. Maybe it still was.

She could almost smell cookies baking and hot chocolate with a peppermint stick to stir it, could almost feel her icy fingers burning from the hot mug.

That child still called out to her, but the contact

had been severed. Sighing, she pressed her forehead to the icy glass and closed her eyes.

Get over it, she told herself. *Just get over it.*

Easier said than done, like so many things in life.

After a few minutes, the windowpane sucked enough warmth from her forehead that it became uncomfortable. She straightened and once again looked out at the snow, wishing she were up at her cabin, where she could be sitting before a crackling fire in the woodstove, while watching the world turn white and the tree branches bend under this new burden.

Giving another sigh, she turned back to face the room. On the floor beside the bed was a huge sack of books. The town bookstore held copies of every new novel they thought she would enjoy, and once a month she picked them up. The library also allowed her to borrow books for longer than the usual two weeks, so she never lacked for reading material. Her tastes were eclectic, running the entire gamut of fiction and non-fiction. Better than television, she always thought.

So, she could go stretch out on that bed with one of her new treasures and read away the rest of the evening, as she would if she were up at her cabin.

For some reason, though, the idea didn't tempt her tonight. She felt too antsy, too uneasy. Ordinarily, when she came into town, she was gone by evening, having finished all her errands and stocked up on food for another month. But the blizzard was keeping her from leaving tonight, much as she wanted to.

And her thoughts kept drifting to Jon Erikson. He was gutted, she thought. Twisted out of all human norms. But of course he had to be, given what he'd probably been doing in Afghanistan. As she knew only too well, some experiences changed you forever.

She cocked her head suddenly, surprised to hear the sound of an approaching engine. Surely even the deputies were off the road now.

Curious, she returned to the window and was amazed to see a Conard County Sheriff's vehicle pull up into a spot right next to her Jeep. The tan Suburban carried a plow blade, as did her Jeep. At this time of the year, anyone who had to travel the back roads had to be prepared to clear the way.

To her amazement, she saw Nate Tate, the sheriff, climb out. Then he reached inside his vehicle and lifted out something wrapped in a blanket. Moments later he was standing at her door knocking.

She opened it immediately, blinking as blowing snow stung her face and eyes. "Nate! What…?"

"Don't ask me," he said, stepping inside and shouldering the door closed. "Talk to Marge."

"Marge?" Why was his wife involved in whatever he was doing?

"This was her idea. I had nothing to do with it. And why she did it now instead of at Christmas, I still don't know. But she said I had to bring it tonight." His weathered face split into a grin. "Of course, I get to see the fun."

"What is it?"

"You'll see." Still grinning, he handed the blanket-wrapped bundle to her.

It squirmed, and she almost dropped it. "Nate!"

"Unwrap the poor bugger before he smothers."

Still gaping with astonishment, she put the bundle on the bed and pulled the blanket away. A Siberian husky pup looked up at her with black-limned, brilliant blue eyes, then plopped on his bottom and let forth an indignant howl. *"Ahrooo!"*

"He's very vocal," Nate said. "Marge calls it singing." His tone left no doubt that he thought otherwise.

Melinda stared, dumbfounded and enchanted all at once. She kept trying to say something, but no words came out.

"Don't worry," Nate said swiftly, as if he expected an objection. "Marge had already started house-breaking him. I've got forty pounds of food, dishes, leashes and everything else, including something called a Dogloo, for this guy. "I'll just go move the stuff into your car."

He hurried out, as if he wanted to avoid an explosion.

Melinda stared at the puppy, who stared back at her with a cocked head.

Shock began to give way to enchantment. Slowly she sat on the edge of the bed, trying not to startle the small creature. After a moment he pranced over to her as well as he could on the mattress and began sniffing. Melinda let him, waiting patiently for him to learn whatever he needed to know about her.

A puppy. A dog. She'd never had a pet before. And she hadn't even thought about getting one. It was something that had never crossed her radar. Yet here she was being intently sniffed by an irresistible bundle of fur. Any moment now, she realized, she was going to fall in love.

Slowly, slowly, the little furball began to warm her somewhere deep inside. When she at last reached out and stroked the silky fur, he made a little sound and rolled over on his back, showing his pink puppy tummy. She smiled. The smile stretched so wide that her cheeks hurt as she reached out and gave him a tummy rub.

By the time Nate reentered the room, she had the puppy on her lap.

"Well," he said, putting his hands on his hips, "I guess maybe Marge didn't make a mistake."

Melinda looked up at him, her eyes stinging. "Thanks, Nate. Thank you so very much."

He nodded. "I'll tell Marge. Honest to God, I didn't have anything to do with this except for following orders. I don't think it's smart to just give a pet to someone without making sure it's okay. But I guess Marge had you figured better than I do."

Melinda looked down at the pup, who was now licking his paws as if he were a cat. "What's his name?"

"That's for you to decide. Let me bring in some things you'll need tonight, then I'll be on my way."

"It's magical, Nate."

His expression grew somber. "Yeah," he said finally. "We all need a little of that."

"Oh!" Remembering suddenly, she looked up from the puppy. "You said I could bring someone to Christmas dinner, right?"

"Of course you can."

"Jon Erikson is back in town. Do you remember him?"

Nate frowned thoughtfully. "Oh. Yeah. I do. He's been gone a while."

"He doesn't look too well, Nate."

"Well, by all means bring him around. Sooner than Christmas, if you want."

"Maybe I will." Without realizing it, she had begun to stroke the puppy's back. Looking down, she saw him yawn, his eyelids heavy.

"Don't let that deceive you," Nate said.

"What?"

"That he's sleepy. That little bugger runs twenty out of every twenty-four hours. My advice? Nap when he does, 'cause that's all you'll get."

Laughing, he went back out to get the things he'd

said she would need tonight. Twenty minutes later, she was alone again.

Only not alone. She had a furry bundle of magic sound asleep on her lap.

She stroked him lightly and said softly, "Hello, Noel."

Chapter 3

Before he left town, Jon stopped by the grocery to gather supplies and ate a hearty meal at the truck stop. He couldn't stand the motel room another minute, and he was too wired to stay in town. He figured the only way to save his sanity was to get out into the countryside. Up in the mountains. The only place he felt comfortable anymore.

Some part of him recognized his behavior as abnormal, yet another part of him recognized that training was difficult to overcome. You couldn't be on a battlefield one day, then step off the plane the next day at home, and expect to feel comfortable and safe immediately. Far from it.

Besides, he was worrying about his guys back in Afghanistan. He needed to be on the move, thinking, dealing with his internal turmoil, not locked up in some stuffy motel room. Nor was he sure he wanted to soften his edge, not when he was going back there in just under a month.

The state highway out of town had already been plowed, but he didn't plan to walk along it very far. He remembered another road that led up to some ranches and then to a forest service road, and he took it. Not that he needed roads. No, man. Back in Afghanistan, he was lucky if he had a goat track he could follow safely.

The early light was washed out beneath a ceiling of dove-gray clouds. The world seemed to have lost its depth and become flat. Even the ridges in the snow were nearly invisible in this light.

But he could see for miles, and that helped calm him. He needed that sphere of emptiness just now.

And the walking felt good. It lulled his demons into silence, and while he remained alert, he also felt calm. On the move. Never holding still.

Survival.

Gradually the slope steepened, and finally he reached the end of the plowed road, near a ranch entrance. Above that the road was marked only by the reflector poles sticking up out of the snowbanks, guides for plows and fools. He walked right between them, the snow knee-deep and exhausting.

He needed the exhaustion. He needed it to silence all the voices and all the visions he had accumulated. Just put one foot in front of the other and *don't think about it*. The warrior's creed. Because the minute you started thinking, you couldn't do what you needed to do.

Sometimes he thought this business of sending people home between tours in-country was a bad deal. They didn't do that in the Second World War. But these days they seemed to think you needed to get away for a while. Maybe you did. It wasn't long enough to truly feel at home again, but it *was* long enough to soften the edge that protected you. It was also the time most guys deserted, because the thought of going back drove them nuts.

And knowing you were going back, you *had* to hang onto things that made you all but unacceptable in regular society.

The devil's dilemma.

As he climbed higher into the quiet mountains, the trees began to close in again, evergreens and leafless aspens, but this time the shortened visual range didn't make him tense. In fact, for once, the climbing truly relaxed him. For a little while he didn't have to be wired. No threatening sounds reached him; no sense of eyes following him bothered him.

Slowly a sense of peace began to infiltrate his body and mind. He shouldn't feel this way. It was dangerous to relax. But he relaxed anyway.

The cold, dry air felt good in his lungs, the higher altitude fresher and more comfortable. He had acclimated to the mountains of Afghanistan so well that only now did he start to feel comfortable physically. The scent of evergreens spiced the air, but he couldn't pick out any of the other scents that always constituted a caution: no smell of wood smoke, food or heavy tobacco. No scent of another human being's unwashed body.

Then, just as his whole being had relaxed into the rhythm of the hike, he heard the distant sound of an engine behind him.

At once he halted and swung around, his eyes immediately searching out places that would provide cover. His hands felt achingly empty without the comfort of his rifle. His right hand went immediately to the hunting knife hanging from his belt.

Wired.

Then it struck him where he was. That engine offered no threat whatever. When it got near, if it did, all he had to do was move to the side and let it pass.

But his heart didn't stop hammering immediately. He turned and forced himself to resume his walk, even though the back of his neck was prickling like mad again.

The engine grew steadily closer, and finally he turned to face it. At once he recognized Melinda's forest service Jeep. It was plowing its way up the road, occasionally straining, but gamely pushing forward. Jon crossed the road so he would be on the far side of the snow she was shoving to the side of the road. Shortly she came up beside him and braked.

"Where are you going?" she asked him.

"Looking for a place to camp."

"Then climb in. There's a campground not too far from my cabin, and it has some important amenities, like water that isn't full of giardia."

He understood her reference immediately. Amoebic dysentery was a problem everywhere in untreated water.

He hesitated only a moment before nodding. "Thanks." He rounded the Jeep, tossed his backpack in the rear and climbed in beside her.

"You should have told me you were coming up this way this morning," she said as she shifted into gear. "I could have saved you the walk."

"I needed it," he said. "But thanks."

"Sure." She tossed him a smile and returned her concentration to the road ahead.

Then Jon felt something move against his hip. Startled, he jumped and twisted, only to find himself looking into a pair of eyes as blue as a summer sky. "What the…?"

"Oh, sorry." She laughed. "I was given a dog for Christmas last night. His name is Noel."

"Uh…cute." Except for the part where his heart had slammed into his throat and every instinct to kill had filled him.

"Sorry he startled you. I should have mentioned he was in here, but I'm so new to having a dog I didn't think about it."

Jon stared down at the dog, which stared solemnly back at him. And then started wagging its tail.

"He's friendly," Melinda said, pressing the accelerator a little harder to gain momentum against a wind drift ahead. "At least I think he is. I doubt Nate Tate would have given me a killer."

"He's too small to kill anything except a mouse. A rat would probably outweigh him."

"Right now."

The Jeep slid slightly sideways then regained traction. The dog, apparently tired of staring at the man who was holding as still as a statue, turned to a more interesting pastime: sniffing him.

Jon tried to ignore the little mammal. There was no room in his life for an attachment, however brief. But there was something about the puppy that wouldn't let him ignore it.

Maybe it was the little animal's intensity. He seemed totally involved in absorbing Jon's scents, whatever they were. Or maybe it was the absolutely unconcerned way the puppy began to crawl onto him, everything about him saying, *I know you won't hurt me.*

"If he bothers you," Melinda said, "just put him in back."

Jon wasn't going to admit that anything so small and harmless could bother him, although his skin was crawling with wariness at letting anything get so close. "He's fine."

He looked out the window, trying to ignore the pup, but that didn't work very well when he felt ten pounds of warmth settle on his lap.

He looked down and saw that Noel had curled up quite comfortably, and his eyelids were hanging at half-mast.

God. The thing trusted him.

"I'm trying to decide," Melinda said, "whether he should be an indoor or an outdoor dog."

"What do you mean?"

"Well, I hear huskies are healthier if they live outdoors. But I'm not sure that doesn't have more to do with their coats getting wet if they come indoors for a while covered with snow. If that happens and you take them back out right away, they'd get awfully cold, don't you think?"

"Probably."

"So I guess, in winter, it's an either-or proposition. I guess, given how young he is and that I don't have any other dogs, it would be better to keep him with me inside most of the time. And just make sure he's dry before we hit the trail."

"Do you walk around out here much in the winter?"

"I have to. We have winter hikers and campers from time to time, and I have to keep an eye on the wildlife. So I hike, snowshoe, ski…whatever's best for where I need to go."

"Sounds nice."

"I love the isolation," she said. "It's so quiet out here. Especially in the winter. It's my favorite time of year. So how come you decided to go camping?"

He hesitated. He wasn't accustomed to talking about himself anymore. And worse, he was certain that she would think he was crazy, which he probably was by now. "I, uh, just don't feel comfortable indoors. When I'm in Afghanistan, I live in the mountains, mostly in caves. I just got used to it."

She nodded as if she understood. "There's a safety in not being in town."

Now what the devil did that mean for her? he wondered, but didn't know how to ask.

"So you don't enjoy the amenities even when you're on leave?" she asked.

"I thought I would. But I'm going back." As if that explained it all. Maybe it did.

She didn't respond, and he was left to wonder if she understood what he meant. Or if even *he* understood it. *Wired.* It was as if he couldn't stop being wired.

After a bit she spoke. "There are some caves on Thunder Mountain. I could show you. Or, if you don't have a tent, I have a spare you can use."

"Thanks." Her acceptance seemed strange to him. He'd half expected her to tell him he was nuts. Instead she was offering to show him a cave if he wanted one.

The last four years didn't mean that he'd forgotten how things were *supposed* to be here. The disjunction felt weird, as if he hadn't left Afghanistan at all, yet he had.

Then the humor of it struck him unexpectedly. Apparently that hadn't deserted him along with the other things that had vanished. He laughed.

She glanced at him. "What?"

"I just thought how ridiculous it sounds, looking for a cave to hide in."

Her lips curved upward, and a chuckle escaped her. "I expect a lot of people would like a cave to hide in."

"Yeah. Of course, for most it's not a compulsion."

"Do you really have to live off the land over there? No bases?"

"Not big bases, although we have some. But believe me, it's safer just to keep moving."

"So do you deal a lot with the locals?"

"All the time. I like most of them a lot. But things are getting worse over there."

"How so?"

"The Taliban are coming back and raiding. We spend a lot of time hunting for their weapons caches, of course, and hunting for them. But they're still rolling into villages and killing people. And they burn a lot of schools, mostly schools for girls."

"God, that's awful."

"We were actually making headway for a while.

Now it feels as if we're losing ground. But it'll turn around again."

"You're very committed, aren't you?"

He didn't think of it that way. "I just do what I have to."

Silence fell again, except for the grind of the Jeep's engine and the crunch of snow against the plow. Half an hour later they came to a halt beside a small log cabin, beneath a slanted roof that served as a carport. Also parked there was a snowmobile, and not too far away was a gas pump.

Noel stirred, sitting up and yawning massively, showing rows of tiny milk teeth. At once he howled.

"I guess he needs a walk," Melinda said. She reached over and scooped him up. "Come on. I'll make us both a warm drink before I show you the campground."

The puppy seemed dismayed by the deep snow at first. He stepped into it, lifting each paw high, as if to keep it clear. It was as deep as he was tall, and for a few moments it appeared he was going to chicken out.

Then, surprising them both into laughter, he nose-dived into the snow and began to burrow into it.

"I guess he really is a husky," Melinda said.

"I hear they stray a lot and can't find their way home."

"What an awful thought." But she didn't run to pick him up. Instead, she let him burrow to his heart's content, and then laughed again when his head popped up out of the snow. Then, with apparent pride, he came back toward the carport, squatted and did his business.

An instant later he leapt into Melinda's arm. She laughed again as he licked her face and led the way into the cabin.

The front room clearly served as both office and living area. There was a counter sporting park brochures and a cash register, and maps decorated the walls. Over to one side were a sofa, an easy chair and a woodstove. Melinda dropped the puppy to the floor, and went to stir up the embers in the stove and add wood. It wasn't long before the fire blazed merrily and warmth began to penetrate the chilly air.

"Have a seat," she told Jon. "I'll get the stuff from my kitchen, and we'll make hot drinks on the stove here."

"Is that where you cook?"

"Naw." She flashed a smile. "I have a propane stove, and a generator if I really need electric power." But she lit an oil lamp before disappearing into the back of the cabin.

Jon took the opportunity to look around. She appeared to lead a very basic lifestyle, one that didn't look as strange to him as it might to others. Most of the world lived like this, or worse. And after the earthquake that had destroyed so much of Kashmir, a lot of them didn't have even this much, although he and his men tried to help out, tried to assist in rebuilding homes.

He finally came to rest on the sofa, figuring the easy chair was probably her favorite, and unzipped his parka. A thump-thump issued repeatedly from the rear of the house, and finally Noel reappeared, skittering to a stop on the bare wood floor, his tongue hanging out and a sappy grin on his face. He looked at Jon, then tore off again, *thump-thump*, on his own private racetrack.

By the time Melinda returned with a teakettle and a coffeepot and set them atop the stove, Jon had removed his parka. The room was warming rapidly. Melinda adjusted the damper, then settled into the armchair. "I'm making both coffee and water for tea," she said. "I didn't know which you'd prefer."

"Either is fine. I'm easy to please."

She gave him a long, thoughtful look. Before she could ask him a question, he decided to forestall her.

"How long have you been doing this?" he asked.

"Since I got out of college about four years ago."

"And you like being alone like this?"

"I like it better than the summers, when I have to deal with all kinds of people." One corner of her mouth lifted. "Is that so surprising?"

He shrugged. "It's just my experience that most people don't like solitude."

"There's a vast difference between solitude and loneliness. I'm not lonely, and I like solitude."

He nodded. "To each his own."

She cocked her head to one side. "You do a very important job, but I'm not sure I could stand it."

He averted his gaze, uncomfortable. Somehow she always managed to turn the subject back to him.

Another turn of the tables. "Did you take special training?"

She nodded. "Forestry school."

"I never got to college."

"When have you had time?"

An unwilling smile escaped him. "Not much since 9/11."

"That's what I thought." She rose as steam began to rise from the kettle. "Tea? Or do you want to wait for coffee? It just started perking, so maybe five minutes or so."

The coffee was starting to smell really good. "I'll wait for the coffee."

She pulled a mug off a nearby shelf, dropped a tea bag into it and filled it with steaming water. Soon the aroma of tea and jasmine reached him. Apparently it reached Noel, too, because he came thumping out of the back of the cabin to wind up at Melinda's feet. She laughed, set her mug on the table by her chair and bent down to lift him up. When she buried her face in the dog's fur, Jon felt something tighten within him. At once he forced the feeling away.

"He's certainly going to keep me busy," she said, lifting her face from the silky fur. The puppy's adult markings were only just hinted at yet, a gray coloration that hinted of his coming mask then ran down along his spine. "I think he wants something to eat, but I left the biscuits in the car."

Jon immediately rose. "Where is his stuff? I'll get it."

"Thanks. It's all in the back of the Jeep. Nate really loaded me down."

He didn't even bother to put on his parka. He needed to go outside and feel the chill. Needed to halt the softening he was beginning to feel within himself. It was a dangerous luxury he couldn't afford until he came home for good. Walls, defenses and habits that had been built so painstakingly since he arrived in Afghanistan the first time had to remain in place for his own safety, both mental and physical.

But, damn, she was a pretty woman, and that dog was nearly irresistible.

She hadn't exaggerated. By the time he carried all the puppy supplies indoors, there was a huge mound by the counter. Noel immediately attacked with his nose, sniffing every little thing until he found the box of biscuits. Then he pawed at it.

"Smart little bugger," Jon remarked.

"Of course," she answered airily. "He's mine."

Jon laughed. "Of course. How stupid of me to remark on it."

Melinda fished out a couple of biscuits and pressed one into Jon's hand. "You give him one, too."

He would have preferred not to, but there was no

gracious way to refuse, so he squatted down and held out the little bone-shaped biscuit. Noel dashed toward him, screeched to a halt that almost tumbled him head over heels, then surprised them both by sitting patiently in front of Jon, although he never took his eyes off the biscuit.

"Nate said his wife had him trained," Melinda said, "but I never imagined he meant to this degree."

"Makes life a lot easier, doesn't it?" Jon gave the biscuit to Noel, who promptly plopped down on his tummy and began to gnaw at it. "He's probably going to want water. Where do I get it, and where do you want me to put the bowl?"

She pulled a stainless-steel bowl out of a shopping bag. "Back here in the kitchen. I'll show you. And by the way, if I'm gone and you need something, you can always get in. I never lock this place."

"Never?"

She shook her head. "Only when I'm here. Otherwise I leave it open. You never know when someone might have an emergency."

But he didn't miss the locked gun safe on the way back to the kitchen. Apparently she had at least one rifle.

"I guess here is best," she said, spreading a towel on a corner of the floor near the sink. The kitchen wasn't very large, and barely had room for a rickety-looking wood table and four chairs. Jon filled the bowl with water and set it on the towel. He felt almost curious to find out how long it would take the puppy to find it.

As he turned from putting the bowl down, he got his answer. In the doorway stood Noel, half a biscuit hanging out of his mouth, watching.

Once again Jon laughed. Melinda joined him.

"It's almost criminal," Jon said, still laughing. "He's too cute."

"I know." She looked rueful. "I never thought of having a pet of any kind, and I wasn't sure I was happy about this one being dumped on me, but before I knew it, he'd wormed his way in."

"Yeah, I can see how he'd do that."

Still holding the biscuit, Noel went to check out the bowl. Satisfied, he ran back to the front room with the two adults following behind him.

"Coffee's ready," Melinda announced. "Do you like anything in it?"

"Black is the only way."

She poured him a mug and he took it in both hands as he would have when sitting around a campfire on a cold night, warming his fingers and letting the warmth run up his arms.

Melinda put the pot on an iron shelf that was built into the back of the stove. "You can usually find a hot pot right there if you want some," she told him. "I've got one going all day when I'm in."

"Thanks. How far away is this campsite?"

She smiled. "Right now, far enough. When it's summer, *not* far enough."

"What do you mean?"

"Oh, just that when the campground is busy, I can hear most everything."

"Are you alone when the place is busy?"

She shook her head. "I usually have two or three forestry students to help out as interns in the summer. Which is good, because sometimes people get drunk and a little disorderly, or they do stupid things and get hurt, or they mistreat the wildlife. I couldn't handle all that alone."

"I wouldn't think so."

"But for the most part, it's a pretty peaceful job. And most people are nice."

That last phrase sounded almost like a mantra to him, and he wondered once again what lay in her past.

But the situation, he decided, was becoming more dangerous by the minute. He was getting to know her and she him, and that wasn't something he wanted to do, with exactly twenty-six days left of his leave. He didn't want to get back to his unit with memories of someone left behind. Not even just a friend. All that did was make things harder.

As soon as he finished his coffee, which was probably indecently quickly, he stood. "Where do I find that campground?"

She, too, rose, and reached for her parka. "It's not

that far if you go through the woods. Do you want to walk the shortcut, or should I drive us over there?"

"Let's walk," he said.

It would leave a smaller trail.

Chapter 4

Jon put his tent up in a matter of minutes, then went to the woodpile Melinda had pointed out to him, brushed off the snow and carried the light, dry wood back. A fire pit was a built-in feature of the campsite, and all he had to do was shovel the snow out of it with his hands and remove the dead leaves beneath. A hole in wet dirt, it was safely ringed by large rocks. Long experience allowed him to get the fire going in a matter of minutes. Then, after spreading a waterproof ground cloth, he sat cross-legged beside the fire and nursed it slowly into a bigger blaze.

This was more like it. He could have brought more conveniences with him, but he wasn't used to them anymore. A scoop of coffee grounds in a tin cup of hot water, a small pan to heat the water in and plenty of MREs just about covered his needs. In fact, the hot water was a true luxury, one he often didn't have in the field, because pans and cups made noise. Too much noise.

It all depended on whether they had a fairly stable base of operations to work out of, and all too often his unit didn't. They'd become so good at blending in and working with Afghans that they were pretty much out on their own most of the time.

Sitting by the fire in the snow, though, took him back to other times and places. He recalled one snowy afternoon when he and his patrol had gathered around a fire like this with a couple of Afghan soldiers. The six of them had been working closely for several months, and had developed the kind of bond men grew when they shared danger together and covered each other's backs. Jon and his guys had taken some courses in the local language before being dumped out there, and experience had made them passably fluent.

One of the rules they usually followed was to avoid the personal. They couldn't afford to be thinking about wives and kids and parents, and developing a bad case of homesickness. Nor, at some level, did they really want to know each other that way. It already hurt bad enough when one of them bought it.

But that night one of the Afghans started the forbidden conversation. At first it had seemed innocuous enough, talk about life before the Russians invaded.

"Hey."

Startled, he looked up and saw Melinda standing there, the pup in her arms.

"I'm sorry, I didn't mean to startle you. I just wanted to make sure you had everything."

She was feeling the solitude, he realized. Maybe he was, too. And he could tell it was odd for both of them. He scooted over on the tarp. "Have a seat. I was just about to make field coffee."

"Throw it in a tin cup and wait for the grounds to settle?" She grinned.

"Exactly. We'll have to share the cup, though."

"No problem. Mr. Speedy Gonzalez here wanted to get out and run."

She settled beside him on the tarp and put the pup down. Noel eyed the fire suspiciously but seemed to realize instinctively that he'd better not get too close. After studying it for a minute, he wandered off to play in the snow.

"You looked lost in thought," she said.

"I was." He hesitated, then decided what the hell. "I was remembering these Afghan soldiers we worked with. There was a snowy afternoon when we'd finished our patrol and decided to enjoy some heat. It looked kinda like it does right now."

"Were they friends of yours?"

"By then, sort of. One of them started talking about

life before the Russians invaded. Those people never had it easy. Some of them still talk about the glory days of the Silk Road, but that was a long time ago. Basically they're a mountain country just scraping by. Everyone wants to pass through, few want to stay. But those who stayed used to at least have a life. Crops, herds, what we'd call subsistence, I guess."

"But not now?"

"Well, the place was never totally peaceful. I'm sure you've heard of the warlords."

"Of course."

He nodded and adjusted the pot of melted snow as the wood beneath it collapsed a little in the blaze, threatening to spill it. "But back in the warlord days, you basically gave your fealty to the nearest strongman, and unless something happened with another warlord, you were protected."

"But now…?"

He shook his head. "The Russians wanted to put a pipeline through. Funny how oil seems to be at the root of everything now. All that black gold gets purchased with red gold. Blood."

"But weren't the locals also in the opium business?"

He looked at her. "I'm never going to criticize a man for doing what he has to do to feed his family."

She hesitated, then slowly nodded. "I can see that."

"Anyway, this guy was sitting there at the fire, talking about the good old days before Russia, before the Taliban, before us. And I listened to him, thinking that wasn't much in the way of good old days, but it sure as hell was better than what they got left with."

"How so?"

"Every village is a front line now. And has been since the Russians. Everyone is fighting for different agendas, and the guys who'd just like to be left alone to raise their goats or their poppies don't get left alone. We walk into a village and start looking for terrorists or weapons caches, and if someone talks to us, he might be dead by sundown. The amazing thing is how many of them help us anyway. They don't want the Taliban back, and now that we've armed the warlords to the teeth, they don't want them, either. As for bin Laden and his crew, they're popular in some places and loathed in a whole lot of others. All these folks want is peace. Instead they got shot in a matter of a few decades from a tribal culture into the full horror of twenty-first-century war."

Melinda sighed and looked into the fire. "That's awful."

"Yeah. It is. Meanwhile, we're trying to get them to establish a national government, which is something they never had before and don't fully understand. And the warlords don't like it at all."

He prodded the fire again and adjusted the pot. It was getting close to a boil.

"All that," she said, "must make it very difficult for you."

"Actually, I don't think about it. I can't afford to."

She turned to him. "But you're thinking about it now."

"It's sitting by this fire. It reminded me. That guy was in his thirties. I don't think he can really remember anything else, but he was repeating the talk of his elders. Most of those people, except for the ones carrying RPGs and Kalashnikovs, would vastly prefer to return to the nineteenth century."

Noel came by, as if to touch home base and reassure himself, then dashed back into the snow, tunneling for a bit, only to pop his head up like a snow gopher. From time to time he howled for some reason known only to him.

"I hope he doesn't draw the wolves," Melinda remarked.

"There are wolves out here?"

"They arrived a few years back. No one knows exactly when, but we figure they must have migrated from Yellowstone. You heard about them being reintroduced there?"

He nodded.

"Well, we've got a pack here. At least one that I'm sure of. It might have split into two by now. I'm trying to track them without disturbing them too much."

"Why are you worried about Noel attracting them?"

"They're not dangerous to humans, but I'm not certain what they'd make of him. It's conceivable he could look about the right size for a snack."

Jon almost chuckled. "Somehow I bet they'd just see him as another puppy. He's not *that* different."

"You're probably right, as long as he doesn't take it into his head to follow them."

At that moment Noel came crashing back to them, sliding into the side of Jon's leg before clambering up into Melinda's lap. He'd apparently had enough of the snow for now.

John poured steaming water into the cup he'd already prepared, then placed it near the edge of the fire to let the grounds steep and settle.

Snow had begun to fall again, gently, and it hissed as it hit the fire. Jon looked at Melinda again and saw that her gaze had grown distant and her face had tightened. He had no doubt she was remembering something unpleasant.

It took him a minute, but he forced himself past his self-imposed reserve. "Are you okay?"

She started, then looked at him. "I'm fine. Sometimes I just remember things I'd rather not."

With that, she pushed herself to her feet, puppy in one arm. "I'm sorry. You said you came out here for solitude, and I invaded. I'll just head back."

She took a couple of steps from the fire, then paused. "I'm going out tomorrow to check for possible avalanche areas. If you want to tag along, I guess that would be okay."

Before he could answer, she was off into the woods, Noel howling his head off.

Jon waited a while, half hoping the wolves would show up, but the woods remained silent and nothing moved.

It could have been the inside of a coffin.

Chapter 5

"Okay," Melinda said to Noel after he'd gobbled down his supper, "it's two weeks until Christmas. We're going to decorate."

Since he'd already found a comfortable spot to curl up on the couch, he evinced disinterest with a big yawn.

"I know, you could care less. But I care. It's not much, but it'll be pretty."

The decorations were up in the cabin's attic, a place that was drafty but managed to get just enough heat from the woodstove to make it tolerable. The hardest thing to get down was the artificial tree she'd bought two years ago, a seven-footer with fiber optic lights. She didn't turn on the lights very often, because that meant starting the generator and she hated to burn fuel for something so inconsequential, but between Christmas and New Year's there were often park visitors who'd come out to cross-country ski and hike, and she liked to turn them on then. It seemed friendlier somehow, and God knew, she had to practice being friendly.

After she'd struggled and banged around, she got the box downstairs and pushed it into the front room. Next there were several boxes of ornaments that glistened enough in the glow from the oil lamps to make up for not lighting the tree. She reminded herself to hang the unbreakable items down low, in case Noel decided to play with them.

Then came a couple of boxes of other things: garlands, a wreath, bows and even bright-red Christmas stockings for no one at all. But they looked nice tacked to the wall.

And finally her most favorite box of all: the Nativity. She'd really splurged on that. All the figures were ceramic and a foot tall. She especially liked the fact that they were darker skinned, too. That felt more realistic to her.

Noel watched all this through drooping eyelids, surprising her once with a small belch.

She looked at him. "I thought dogs didn't do that."

He yawned as if to say, *And what do you know about dogs?*

"Good point. Did anyone ever tell you that you're *too* cute?"

He settled his chin on his paws, looking at her.

"Yeah, probably a million times already, and you're what…three months old? If that?"

His steady gaze never wavered, although his eyelids were beginning to sag again.

"Nate was right about you. You'll be bouncing around again in an hour. Maybe I should nap. You sure didn't let me get a lot of sleep last night."

One of his ears twitched in response, then *snap,* his eyelids closed.

That easy chair did look good, Melinda thought. She scanned the waiting boxes and decided there was no rush. Instead she settled in her chair, put her feet up and stared at the blaze through the glass door of her woodstove.

Nice. Very nice.

Her own eyelids drooped, and moments later she was sound asleep.

The sound of howling and the rapid thump of feet awoke her abruptly. The oil lamp had burned out, and the fire was now little more than a red glow of coals. She could barely make out Noel running in excited circles, howling his fool head off.

Well, at least it had been more than an hour, she thought, as she struggled to shed her dream and find the will to move.

"Ahwooo!"

"Okay, okay." What did he want now? Another walk?

Noel raced in frantic circles, colliding with boxes and walls but barely noticing, as if he were a ball in a pinball machine.

"Ahwooo!"

She pushed herself to her stockinged feet and headed for her boots, which were beside the door, beneath the hook for her parka. "Cool your jets, little man. I'm coming."

The radio crackled to life before she could shove her feet into her boots, and Nate Tate's voice filled the room.

"Melinda? Are you there? Over."

Sliding a bit in her stocking feet, she crossed to the desk behind the counter and lifted the microphone to her mouth, pressing the talk button. "I'm here, Nate. The howling you hear in the background is my Christmas present. I think he needs a walk."

"I won't keep you long. I just wanted to alert you. We had a bank robbery today, and the perp shot one of the tellers."

"Who?" Melinda's heart slammed. She knew most of the tellers, many from her school days.

"Charlene Jansen. She's okay. She was lucky. A little patchwork and she'll be fine."

Physically, Melinda thought. She would be fine physically, but what about emotionally? "Thank God."

"That's the first thing, but you also need to know that someone just saw the perp's truck on the county road headed west toward your general area. I don't see why he should come anywhere near you, because if he wants to get away he'd be smarter to turn south on County Road 33. But on the off chance he decided to duck into the mountains, I want you to be on the lookout, okay?"

She tensed. "Yeah. I'll watch out."

"Carry your weapon, Melinda. This guy is armed."

"I will."

"I'll keep you posted. Out."

A sharp rap on the door caused her to freeze. Now she knew what had Noel so stirred up. It was late, though, and dark as pitch outside, and nobody ought to be banging on her door.

Concerned and fearful, she changed tack and went to the kitchen. In a drawer, behind the silverware trays, she kept her service revolver. By feel, she released the safety. She didn't have to check whether it was loaded.

Then, moving quietly, she returned to the front door. Noel was now standing still, looking at her as if to say, *I did my job. Now do yours.*

Her heart thudded in her chest. There had been a time when she'd been alone and had opened a door and…

Not now! she told herself sternly. Don't think about it.

But whether or not she thought about it, the fear still sent her adrenaline through the roof. Pistol in her right hand, she reached out with her left to turn the knob on the heavy, old-fashioned dead bolt. It released with a *thunk*.

Then she lifted the iron latch and slowly opened the door, the pistol pointing at whatever was out there.

"Oh my God," she gasped. It was Jon Erikson.

He looked from her face down to her nearly invisible pistol. It was snowing again, and the night was only slightly brighter outside than in. To her, he was little more than a silhouette. "You come loaded for bear, huh?" he said, not so much as twitching a muscle.

Slowly she flipped the safety on and lowered the pistol. "Sorry. There's an armed bank robber on the loose, and I've got to be careful out here on my own."

"Sure, I understand."

He seemed to, she realized. "Do you need something?"

"The, uh, outdoor facilities are locked."

"Oh! I clean forgot." She stepped back and motioned him in. Noel at once started dancing around his feet and sniffing. She couldn't help but notice that he tried to ignore the puppy.

"I'm sorry," she continued as she closed the door behind him. "We lock the outhouses in the winter, ever since that little girl in Colorado was kidnapped and dumped in one."

"I remember that. She was lucky those hikers came by."

"Yeah. Very lucky. So when the campground isn't busy, we lock them. Here, let me show you mine. It's more comfortable, anyway, and warmer. You're welcome to use it any time."

"Thanks." One corner of his mouth lifted, just visible in the glow from the stove. "Somehow I didn't think you'd want me to dig a hole."

At that she had to grin. "Nope. Absolutely not. Gotta protect the groundwater."

She *did* have the convenience of running water and a flush toilet. She also had a shower, but unless she turned on the generator, it was a very *cold* shower. She'd gotten used to taking sponge baths most of the time, using a pot of water steaming on the woodstove.

She lit another oil lamp and showed him the way, leaving him with the lamp. Then she tucked her pistol back into its hiding place and lit several more lamps in the front room. Now the place looked welcoming again, instead of like a cave on the edge of hell's brimstone. The red eye of the dying fire no longer dominated.

Squatting, she opened the stove door and threw in a couple more logs.

When Jon returned to the front room, he eyed all the boxes. "What's this?"

"Christmas decorations."

"Wow." Something in his gaze grew faraway. "You have no idea how long it's been."

She waited, letting him follow whatever path memory was taking, then offered, "You can help me with them, if you'd like. I sure wouldn't mind."

Slowly he came back to her. "I'd like that," he said quietly. "I'd like that a whole lot."

"I'm not sure I want to start tonight, though. I meant to, but then I fell asleep." She glanced at the pendulum clock on the wall and nearly gasped at the time. Past ten already.

"I'm sorry I woke you."

She ran her fingers through her long, dark hair, pushing it back from her face. "No, that's okay. It was just a nap, and I'd have had to get up soon to walk the dog anyway."

She looked at him, at his blond hair, shaved so close, what the Marines called "high and tight," if she remembered correctly. His eyes, she thought, were green, but the light wasn't good right now, and she couldn't really remember.

"How," she asked unexpectedly, unable to stop the question as it tumbled out, "do you manage to pass in Afghanistan?"

He grew very still, then visibly relaxed. "You've seen pictures. Men there cover their heads."

"But your beard…is that blond, too?"

"Yeah, but I don't grow it out."

"I thought beards were required."

He shrugged. "Under the Taliban, yes. But after the Taliban, a lot of men took great delight in shaving."

She nodded. "Sorry. I don't mean to pry. It just suddenly struck me…"

"I know. My Swedish heritage pretty much sticks out. But I don't often have to pass as anything other that what I am."

Feeling embarrassed, as if she'd made a major faux pas, she invited him to sit. "I think I want some fresh coffee," she said. "Join me?"

Again he hesitated, then nodded. "Sure. Just promise me you'll give me the key to the facilities when I leave."

In that instant the whole wary mood lifted and she was able to smile again. "It's a deal. But first let me walk Noel."

The dog was sitting by the door, his eyes pleading with her.

"I'll do that," Jon said, surprising her. He scooped the pup up in one large arm and took him out.

By the time he returned, Melinda had the coffee perking on the stove and was seated on the edge of her chair. It had just occurred to her that she was showing a remarkable amount of trust in a man she had just met. Ordinarily she was skittish around strange men, sometimes even panic-stricken. Could her memories of Jon in high school be sufficient to counter all that had happened since then?

Maybe so. Or maybe it was something about him.

For all that he tried to seem distant and reserved, there was something else, something that seemed to promise safety. Something that said he was by nature a protector.

An odd thing to think about a man whose job probably involved killing people. Yet she was sure, at some deep gut level, that he would never hurt *her*. Very few men had ever made her feel that way. In fact, giving it some thought, she realized she felt that way about Nate Tate and his deputy Micah Parish, and no one else.

But then, they were the ones who'd found her, who'd saved her. But for Micah's skill at tracking…

She quickly jerked her mind back from that precipice. If she went there, it might be hours before she could return to the stability she had managed to create over the last ten years.

Jon was sitting on the couch now, leaving her alone in her thoughts, absently stroking Noel as if he weren't even aware that he was doing it. His eyes were on the flames dancing behind the glass door of the stove. He had given her privacy for her thoughts without even being asked.

But maybe he also wanted privacy for his. He must have far more ugly memories than she did. Quietly she scooted back in her chair and put her feet up. The sense of comfort she had felt earlier as she dozed off with the dog returned, as if it had never been interrupted.

After a bit Jon rose and took two cups down from the hooks on the wall behind the stove. He filled both of them with coffee, asking, "You like anything in yours?"

"No, thanks. It takes too much effort to keep milk and cream up here, and I hate that powdered stuff."

"Me too." He passed her a mug with a half smile, then resumed his seat beside the dog. Noel nestled in contentedly.

"He's adopted you," she remarked.

"Not for long."

He wanted no attachments, she realized. Like her. Solitude wasn't merely comfortable, it was *safe*. "So you have to go back at the end of your leave?"

He nodded.

"For how long?"

He turned his head, gave a little shrug. "Probably for the rest of my career, the way things are going over there."

"Do you think we're really helping?"

"There? Actually, I do. Some of them would prefer the Taliban, of course, but most of them just want to go back to the times before the Russians invaded. The only hope we have of giving that back to them is to restrain the warlords and the Taliban."

"Will that ever happen?"

"I think so, but I can't say when. It's a big leap these people are trying to make. But I told you that."

She nodded and sipped her coffee. "Do you like anything about it over there?"

He surprised her with a smile and a nod. "Actually, I do. People are people the world over, and there's a lot of really nice folks in Afghanistan. I'd like to see women treated better, but that will come with time." He shook his head. "There's one story that upsets me, though. The Taliban invaded a small village not too long ago and burned the girls' school. They threatened the life of the teacher, too. So now classes are being held in some village elder's home, and the teacher travels to and from the school wearing a burkha so she can't be identified, and her brothers go with her to protect her."

"That's awful!"

"And that's the kind of thing I want to see the end of. That's why I'm in those mountains hunting Taliban."

"So it's a good cause."

"I think so."

But she didn't want to imagine the price he was probably paying.

"Enough about that," he said, rising. He refilled his mug and paced around the room. "I'm supposed to be on leave. Away from all that."

"I'm sorry."

He shook his head. "Don't be. There's a large part of me that can't leave Afghanistan anyway. And common sense tells me it would be dangerous if I start relaxing, since I have to go back. I need to keep my edge."

He paused and looked at her, trying to smile. "On the other hand, there still has to be some way to refresh myself."

She didn't know what to say or to suggest. "Do you think you'll get refreshed sleeping in the snow?"

"Maybe. Maybe that's all I need. To see the mountains as a friend again, rather than as a potential enemy."

"Well, if the snow lets up, we can do something about that tomorrow. I've got an extra pair of Nordic skis left by the last ranger. They'd probably be just about right for you. Like I said, you can help me hunt for avalanche hazards."

"I wouldn't know what in the world to look for."

She smiled. "I can teach you."

"What do you do if you find something risky?"

"Post it. It takes professionals to come out here and detonate the dangerous slides. I just try to keep everyone, myself included, away from them."

"Sounds like a good rule for life in general."

She nodded, thinking that indeed it did. But life still set traps, and no matter how many dangerous areas she identified, there was always the chance that she would miss one. And one was all it took.

Chapter 6

The morning dawned with the brightness that could come only with a fresh snowfall reflecting the sun. Blindingly bright, so bright that she needed her protective sunglasses with their mirrored tops and bottoms.

Noel seemed to like the change in weather, prancing and leaping and jumping in the snow like a dervish at top speed. He started barking, and the sound soon brought Jon out of the forest. He looked ready to go, except for ski shoes. Luckily the last ranger had left a pair of those behind, too. They were an almost perfect fit, and before long they were skiing away from her cabin toward the steeper mountain slopes.

Avalanche hazard signs were permanently posted in most places, so Melinda's task was to mark them with caution tape if she felt the danger was high. After her survey, she could post a sign at her cabin announcing the level of danger. In theory, at least, nobody went anywhere in the park without checking in with the ranger, purely for safety reasons. So far this winter she hadn't had any trouble with people ignoring that precaution.

For now, as they followed a hiking trail through the woods, she allowed Noel to scamper around them and wear himself out. When they approached the danger zones, she would leash him, or tuck him into her backpack.

From the sounds of Jon moving behind her, she could tell he was enjoying himself. He kept pace steadily, and the woods were filled with the *swish-swish* of their skis on snow.

Just about the time Noel began to lag, they were approaching the first danger spot. Melinda halted, and Jon came up beside her.

"Not far," she said to him. "In another five minutes or so, we'll be above the trees."

He nodded, and took the opportunity to dig his poles into the snow and squat.

"You're not getting blisters, are you?" she asked.

"I don't think I'm capable of blistering anymore." He glanced at her, his mouth curved wryly. "I'm one great big callus."

She tried not to read any more into that statement than he probably meant. Noel came over to her, no longer prancing, and curled up at her feet, evidently ready to nap.

"I wish I could do that," she said. "Just curl up in the snow and be comfortable."

"You'd need a fur coat."

"Would that be so bad?" She released the clasps on her skis and stepped out of them. The puppy lifted his head and watched.

She swung her backpack off her shoulders and dug into it, pulling out some dog biscuits and a couple of energy bars. She passed one of the bars to Jon.

"Thanks."

Noel poked at the biscuits with his nose, then flipped them through the air with a quick jerk of his head. Then he was off, hunting them down.

"I guess," Jon observed, "he needs to kill them first."

Melinda laughed. "Maybe so. I'm kind of surprised, actually. I didn't realize watching a dog could be so entertaining. I mean, I watch wild animals all the time. I'm fascinated by their habits, and keeping an eye on them is part of my job. But I never thought of dogs as being just as interesting."

"Clearly you've never had one before."

"Have you?"

He nodded, his gaze following the puppy. "In another life. One of the things that fascinates me about them is the way they make a bridge between us and the rest of the wild. You can still see the wolf in them, but you can also see the human."

She squatted, her back against a tree, and looked at him. "The human?"

"We breed them to serve our needs, so of course they reflect us to some extent." He crumpled the foil wrapper from his energy bar in the palm of his hand and tucked it into one of his parka pockets. "Think about it. From all I've read, wolves are basically shy and retiring when it comes to people. They kill only to eat. Dogs, on the other hand, are far more aggressive in general. They'll even bite the hand that feeds them. We've bred that into them. Hardly surprising, when you look at our species."

"Well, we kind of depend on them for some things. Like protection."

"That's one of the things, yes. So instead of slipping away into the forest when something unwanted approaches, they'll bark, face it down, even attack to protect us."

She looked at Noel, who had just "killed" and eaten his first biscuit and was now hunting for the other.

"I hadn't thought of it that way before."

"I'm not saying it's a bad thing. Dogs help us out in lots of ways, and have for a long time. Watch a good herding dog at work, then try to imagine life for the shepherd without him. It's just…" He hesitated. "Well, I guess it's just weird that we're so scared of wolves when we've created more of a monster."

At that she had to nod. "I agree there. Although it's hard to think of it that way just now."

He surprised her with a laugh. "Oh, Noel has me terrified, can't you tell?"

She joined his laughter as the pup, having eaten his second biscuit, returned to her. She hooked the leash on him then and stepped back into her skis. "This could be interesting."

"Just move slowly. He'll figure it out. He's bright."

He was, too. Once he figured out that he wasn't supposed to pull her, he settled down to trotting alongside. Apparently the biscuits had energized him enough to enter hyperdrive again.

Fifteen minutes of steady skiing brought them to the edge of the treeline. Melinda needed only one look to tell her just how dangerous the snowfall was. The wind had even blown the snow on the upper slope into an overhang that would probably come crashing down at any moment. Squatting, she sifted the snow through her fingers, checking its texture.

"Bad?" Jon asked.

"Very."

Straightening, she looked around for the sign. It was buried beneath the snow, only one corner poking out. Handing Noel's leash to Jon, she skied cautiously over and began to dig it out with her hands. Moments later, Jon joined her.

"It's really unstable," she said quietly. "I'll need to ask the patrol to get out here and blast it loose before the holidays.

"I could just shout," Jon suggested.

She gave him a sour look, and he grinned.

"Or maybe Noel will howl."

But the dog seemed suddenly disinclined to bounce around and make noise. He was sitting very, very quietly.

"He senses it," Jon said. "Huskies are supposed to be really good at sensing danger."

"You're not making me feel any better."

"I just mean that you might want to think of him as an early-warning sensor when you're out here on the snow."

With the sign uncovered, she tied caution tape around it and began to string it up the edge of the treeline, wrapping it around a trunk to hold it in place. Jon stretched the tape down the slope and across the bottom of a large bowl-shaped indentation in the rock. She appreciated the help.

Well before the light began to wane, they had marked two other areas of serious concern.

"Are there any more?" Jon asked.

"None that I can get to without spending a couple of nights on the trail. But given the instability of what we've already checked, I think I'll have to close the park until I can get the demolition team out. It's bad now, and if we have another heavy snowfall, it'll be truly deadly out here."

"Yeah."

She looked at him, taking in his cheeks ruddy with the cold and the sparkle that had come to his eyes. Something in her seemed to stop short, with a kind of wonder, and then she felt something she had thought she would never feel again: attraction.

At once she looked down, afraid he would see the sudden hunger on her face. She couldn't allow that.

He bent and scooped up the puppy, managing to tuck him into the warmth of his parka, and then zipping it up so only the dog's head stuck out. "Poor little guy is tuckered out."

"I'm surprised he didn't get tuckered out a long time ago."

He flashed a smile, a surprisingly winning one. "Huskies are made for this. Their endurance is legendary."

Skis on again, they headed back toward the cabin. "Do you have avalanches in Afghanistan?"

"Sure. They're part of being in the mountains. With time, most folks have learned to live out of the way of the majority of them, though."

"And I doubt they ski for pleasure."

A laugh escaped him. "They're smart. They stay at home. Unless they're fighting."

"Some of the folks who come up here on holiday

aren't so smart. We don't have an official ski slope, but they can't resist getting out there in the open areas anyway."

"Do you have to rescue many?"

"Not in a couple of years now. Unfortunately, if someone goes out very far, they're apt to be dead before I realize something is wrong."

"So you try your best to keep them out of the open areas?"

"Absolutely. I warn and warn and warn."

They settled into the easy rhythm of skiing on their way back toward the cabin. Melinda felt as if the world had become timeless. The sun didn't seem to move, and the clouds she occasionally glimpsed gathering over the peaks seemed to grow no bigger.

Out here like this, she usually felt at her most peaceful, but now something was different. Now she had noticed Jon Erikson as a man. Her emotions roiled internally like building storm clouds. She didn't want this. She most especially didn't need this. Long ago she had decided to live her life essentially as a hermit, meeting the rest of humanity on her own terms as much as possible. It was the only safety she knew.

Now this man had intruded. To be fair, she had invited him to intrude for reasons she couldn't begin to fathom. She hadn't needed to suggest they have dinner together at Maude's. She hadn't needed to offer him a ride or invite him to help with the Christmas decorations.

So the question became: what had gotten into her? The recognition of another wounded soul? The world was full of wounded souls.

In the end, she wasn't in the best of moods when they reached the cabin. As if he sensed it, Jon put the pup down, let him do his business, then tucked him inside the front door.

"See you," he said casually, and headed off toward his camp.

That made her feel worse than anything could have. She stood there watching him disappear and wondered why she seemed to have nothing to say.

Chapter 7

Two days later, utterly without warning, another blizzard swept into the mountains. It had come racing down from Canada, according to her radio communications with another ranger station, and it was moving fast and hard. In almost no time at all, Melinda watched the thermometer outside her window drop to twenty-seven below.

"It's a bad one," Larry Bluhfeld told her. "Radio will probably go out, so are you prepared?"

"Always."

"Me too. I'll try to check back with you every couple of hours, but with all this snow blowing, it might not work real well."

"I'll be fine, Larry. Will you?"

He laughed, his voice breaking up on the airwaves. "I've been doing this a long time, Mel. It's my favorite weather. Makes me feel like an old mountain man."

A burst of static filled the room, then Larry's voice came through again. "You're keeping an eye out for that bank robber, aren't you?"

Melinda almost smiled. Larry was like a mother hen sometimes. "As much as possible, but, Larry, honestly, how likely is it he'd come here?"

"I talked to Nate a while ago. He said he was going to radio you again, too. Did he?"

"Not yet."

"Well, he's getting concerned the guy might have come up into the mountains, because there's no sign of him anywhere else, and they had roadblocks out almost as soon as it happened."

"Okay." Melinda felt an uneasy quiver in her stomach but forced herself to ignore it. "I'll be watchful. Did Nate say anything about Charlene?"

"She's home and talking about going back to work. And the bank is installing bulletproof glass around the teller's cage."

"I never thought we'd come to that here."

Another burst of static disrupted the transmission, and Larry's voice never came back.

Melinda turned off the radio to conserve the battery pack and went to stand at the window, looking out. Just now it was reminiscent of being inside a snow globe. Noel snuffled around her ankles, and she looked down at him. "But you just went!"

His unwavering blue eyes peered up at her.

Jon Erikson. She hadn't seen him since they'd skied out to the avalanche danger areas, and she hadn't sought him out. Distance had seemed like the best choice. But with this clipper blowing in from the Arctic, could she leave him out there in nothing but a tent?

Conscience pricked her until at last she suited up in her survival gear and set out to get him. Like it or not, Noel was confined to the cabin. She didn't need to worry about him, as well.

The woods had grown dark, since the storm cut out most of the light, but the trail was still clear. Of course, she knew it by heart, anyway.

Ten minutes later she reached the campsite. The fire was out, buried in snow. Her heart climbed to her throat, and she approached the tent cautiously. "Jon? Jon? Are you there?"

For interminable seconds, no one answered her. Then the flap of the tent opened a slit and his face peered out. "I'm hunkered down for the blow. What the hell are you doing out here?"

"Worrying about you. Come back to my cabin. This is going to be a really bad one."

"I got that feeling." But he didn't move.

"Come on," she said. "My conscience won't rest if I leave you out here."

Another half minute passed; then finally he nodded. "You go on back. I need to gather up a few things."

"Are you sure?"

"That I'll come? Yeah. No point staying out here if there's a warm fire somewhere else."

"Okay." Satisfied, she turned and trekked back toward the cabin. When she stepped inside, Noel acted as if she'd been gone for a month. He'd also made good use of the time, gnawing the corner off one of the Christmas boxes and scattering cardboard everywhere.

She looked down at him, wondering how she could scold him now when he was doing nothing wrong. Instead the little devil was looking up at her from adoring eyes, his tail thumping the floor with delight.

"Sheesh," she said, and scooped him up into her arms. He immediately started licking her face. "How am I ever going to train you if you only misbehave when I'm not around?"

He howled, as if that were a stupid question, then licked her again.

"Come on, I need to get out of these clothes."

Windproof parka with a snorkel hood, windproof snow pants, wool-lined boots, gloves, goggles. It was a relief to get out of them and hang them from their hooks just outside her bedroom. What felt comfortable outside was miserable inside.

Wearing thick socks, jeans and a sweater, she

returned to the front room and checked the fire. It was burning well, not too hot, although the wind required her to adjust the flue a bit. Nearby, her wood box held enough logs for a couple of days. No reason to go out again.

The wind gusted, and ice clattered against her windowpane. Noel looked startled and jumped up onto the couch, curling deep into the throw pillows. Almost laughing at him, Melinda decided to turn on her battery-operated CD player. Some Christmas carols should help cover the storm sounds.

The strains of the Canadian Brass filled the room with cheerful sound, holding the winter storm at bay. The Christmas decorations still sat in their boxes, but she felt not the least urge to put them up.

Instead, she curled up in her chair and closed her eyes, drinking in the music, seeking the spirit of the season. It had to be here somewhere.

The CD was just drawing to a close with the haunting sounds of "Silent Night" when Jon knocked on the door. She leapt up at once, nearly tripping over Noel, who was now running in excited circles, howling his little head off. When she unlatched the door and opened it, she stared dumbstruck at the world outside.

"Whiteout," she said, amazed.

"Yeah, I almost got lost." He shook the snow off himself and stamped his boots to clear them before entering. "It's getting worse by the second."

"What took you so long?"

"My tent blew down, which made it a little hard to gather up my stuff." He smiled and shrugged. "Hence my sincere gratitude for your offer of shelter."

"Nobody should be out in this. Even Eskimos would be inside."

"I think you're right." He began to strip off his outerwear, considerably hindered by a dog under-foot. He didn't seem to mind, though, and eventually got down to his sweatshirt, jeans and socks. Then he scooped up the puppy and settled on the couch. "Did I hear music?"

"I was playing some Christmas carols."

"It's been a long time since I heard any."

"I don't imagine they're real popular over there."

"Not exactly."

Obliging him, she replaced the first CD with one by Mannheim Steamroller.

"God, I've missed that," he said. He stretched his legs out in front of him and let his head rest against the back of the couch. "I ought to take a copy of that back with me."

"It's beautiful," she agreed. Forcing herself to look away, she headed for the kitchen to get some cider to heat with a bit of cinnamon. The stove ordinarily warmed the entire cabin without difficulty, but the kitchen was chilled now, as if not even the thick logs could prevent heat from being sucked out by the storm. She lit a couple of oil lamps and pulled a gallon of cider out of the larder.

She poured the entire gallon into a stew pot, tossed in a few cinnamon sticks and a couple of cloves, and carried it out to the front room, where she put it on the stove.

Jon was sound asleep, the dog curled on his flat belly. She paused, drinking in the sight as if she'd somehow been hungry for it, noting the cleanly chiseled lines of Jon's face, a face that spoke of hardships she could only imagine. Something she'd been ignoring for days ignited deep within her, terrifying her.

She fled back to the kitchen, where, with only the golden light of the oil lamps to drive away the darkness, she clung to the edge of the counter and tried to batter back the memories.

For so long she'd kept them locked safely away, aware that they existed, but not letting them touch her. All of a sudden they were forcing themselves into reality again, filling her with dread and anger and a million other emotions that had driven her to this hermitage in the woods.

Her hard-won peace shattered around her as if a picture window had been punctured, glass flying everywhere, and with it her composure, her safety and all her carefully constructed defenses.

Her fingers tightened on the counter's edge until they ached. She pressed her forehead into the upper cabinet as hard as she could. But despite her every effort, tears began to roll down her cheeks.

Precious things had been stolen from her, and

sometimes—just sometimes—mourning overwhelmed her.

"Melinda?"

Jon's voice, quiet and cautious, reached her from behind.

"Go away," she said, hating the way her own voice broke.

He didn't speak again, but he must have moved very silently, because she felt his heat behind her, a stark contrast to the rest of the kitchen.

"Don't touch me!" She almost shrieked the words, and then the tears started to roll like rivers and...

He didn't listen. Before she could even try to twist away, he had wrapped his arms around her like steel bands, turning her and pressing her face-first into his chest. She struggled against him, but he seemed impervious.

Panic filled her. She struck out with everything she could move, her feet, her fists, her head, yet he never even flinched.

Trapped!

But she had never been trapped like this before. Before it had been ropes and duct tape. Before it had hurt. Jon wasn't hurting her at all. Unyielding, yes, but he absorbed her blows and never once hurt her back.

He just stood solid as rock and let the panic, terror and pain run through her. She cried, she screamed, she swore at him, but not *really* at him, and he seemed to know it.

A long, long time later, exhaustion left her weak as a kitten.

Then, and only then, did he shift his hold on her, lifting her gently in his arms and carrying her out to the front room. He sat on the couch with her in his lap. Moments later Noel scrambled up onto her and licked at her salty tears.

The storm outside still raged, but the one inside had quieted. Melinda felt utterly numb, as if she had not a single feeling left in her. Zombielike, she stared at the fire. She didn't even raise a hand to pet the puppy.

But slowly, very slowly, strength began to seep back into her limbs. The internal deadness lasted longer, which was fine. She didn't care if she ever felt anything again.

But life was rarely so kind. Embarrassment began to creep into her cheeks, and finally she *had* to get off Jon's lap. The position was too intimate. Too welcome. That frightened her, too.

He helped her sit up beside him, never looking at her, giving her the privacy her recent actions seemed to demand.

Wiping the last of the sticky tears from her face with the sleeve of her sweater, she went to the stove. "Cider? It's spiced."

"I'd love some."

She reached for the metal dipper on the wall and filled two mugs. She gave him one, then hesitated only a moment before choosing to sit by him on the couch, rather than in her habitual place in the easy chair.

Noel looked at her for a moment, then curled up on the rug before the fireplace. Outside, the storm's battering seemed to grow.

Jon spoke quietly. "Want to talk about it?"

"No. Yes. I can't." As the words burst out of her in short spurts, she started shaking again.

He didn't say anything. Instead, he went to the fire, stepping carefully over Noel, and put on another log. "It's getting drafty in here."

It was, although she couldn't have said whether the room was really chilling, or if the chill came from within her.

Just then, under the burden of heavy snow, a tree limb broke with the deafening crack of a gunshot.

In an instant she saw Jon's transformation into a warrior. He whirled in the direction of the sound, reaching for a weapon he didn't have.

She saw then the hunter—and the prey—he had become. She saw the metamorphosis in the blink of an eye. It should have scared her, but somehow it increased her trust in him.

She waited, watching him unknot one muscle at a time. "Tree limb," he said.

"Yes."

Nodding, he returned to the couch and reached for his cider. "Sorry."

"No need." And for some reason, now she felt as

if she could talk. "My parents owned a ranch north of town," she said.

"I kind of remember. Vaguely."

"Yeah. Dad raised cattle mostly. I used to love to ride the horses. In fact, like most girls, I was a horse nut."

He didn't say anything, just gave her the space she needed to talk.

"Anyway, I was alone at the house one day. Mom and Dad had gone into town to get some groceries, and being fifteen, I decided I'd rather stay home and listen to my music. I was so *above* those ordinary things. If it didn't involve a gang of my friends, I didn't want to go."

"I remember feeling that way."

She nodded, compressing her lips tightly. "Someone knocked at the door. Around here, you don't worry about things like that. I thought it was somebody looking for work, or one of the hands needing something. Never entered my head it could be anything else."

She sensed him shift toward her, but the move was subtle, so she didn't feel as if she had to shift away. "Anyway, it was a creep. I fought him, but he still got me banged up so that I couldn't see straight, and the next thing I clearly remember was being tied up and gagged in the bed of his pickup truck, hidden under a canvas tarp that smelled…awful. Like something had died in it."

That had terrified her, she realized now. More than being kidnapped, that horrible scent of death had seemed to set a seal on her fate.

His hand settled on her shoulder reassuringly. She didn't shrug it away. For some reason she needed it.

"I figured I was dead," she continued, her voice breaking. "I don't know how long we drove, but the ride got bumpier and bumpier. All I could think of was what he was going to do to me and the shallow grave I was probably going to wind up in. I thought about my parents, and how terrified and upset they were going to be, and I got pissed because they'd never know what happened."

She felt rather than saw him nod.

"You don't need all the details," she said finally. "Eventually the truck stopped. I have no idea where I was, but there was a broken-down cabin. And this *freak* figured he could turn me into his wife. He said I just needed some breaking, like a wild horse."

"God."

A shudder tore through her. Needing to move, she pushed herself off the couch and began to pace. "I don't talk about this," she said, her voice cracking. "I don't *think* about this anymore."

"But it still haunts you."

"Yes. Of course. Some ghosts never go away."

"How long before they found you?"

She broke stride, then resumed her pacing, wrapping her arms tightly around herself. "He had me for nearly three weeks. It was…barbaric. He treated me like an animal he had to tame, and he wasn't nice about it. One time he hit me so hard he broke my cheekbone. The only thing he didn't do was rape me."

"Damn!"

"I was covered with bruises. He wouldn't feed me or give me water unless I did what he wanted, and I was chained all the time. But then…one day…"

A shudder ripped through her again, and she stopped, facing a wall, looking into the past like a tunnel, seeing what was no longer there.

"One day," she said again, her voice growing flat, "he went away. To get supplies, I guess. But he'd been feeding me so little that I'd lost a lot of weight. It took me two hours, and I shredded the skin on my ankle, but I got out of the shackle. Then I stole some heavier clothes—God, they stank, but I didn't care—and some boots, grabbed some food and made a bundle out of a blanket, and I took off.

"God," he said softly.

She turned slowly, looking at him, hollow-eyed. "I hid out in the woods for six weeks, scared to death he'd track me. I never stopped moving. Then one day I came on a couple of women hikers. Right after that, Nate and Micah found me." She shrugged. "They got me back to a ranger station. I spent some time in the hospital, and a lot more time in therapy. But the truth is, Jon, I still only feel safe when I'm out in the woods."

He nodded, his eyes never leaving hers. "Believe me, I understand."

And for some reason, she believed he did. Slowly the tension began to seep out of her. She looked at Noel, still sleeping happily before the fire, then again at Jon. "I usually avoid men," she said, not understanding why she felt it necessary to tell him." Men I don't know, I mean."

"I'd be surprised if you didn't."

"And I've never told this whole story to anyone but the police, the court and my therapist."

He nodded. "I've told you things I never talk about, too. Maybe we both recognize each other's gutted soul."

Slowly she came back to the couch and sat, facing him. "But are we really gutted souls? Do you believe that?"

"Sometimes I think so. Me, at least. Not you. You didn't do anything wrong. I just meant you were seriously harmed."

"But you," she persisted. "What about you?"

"I'm a Marine."

"And?"

"I'm a trained killing machine. I'm not supposed to think about anything except my mission and my buddies."

"Why?"

"Because compassion would get in the way."

She nodded, facing the ugliness square on. He gave her credit for that.

"But you feel it anyway, don't you?"

"Yeah. I do."

She sighed, and astonished him by reaching out to take his hand. "I'm sorry, Jon. The few, the proud, the brave… You're all those things. The terrible part is… well, it's like Nate Tate said to me once. He said, 'When your country calls, the only answer is *Yes, sir.*'"

"At least in Afghanistan I feel like I'm doing some good."

She nodded and squeezed his hand. "You are. Generations of women who get to go to school are going to thank you."

"I hope so."

Silence fell between them, but she continued to hold his hand.

Noel stirred, stretching and yawning, then rubbing his face with his paws. He needed only a second to judge the situation, and he wasted no time leaping up onto the sofa. He squirmed into the space between them, shoving with his nose until he was satisfied with the arrangement, then settled in.

Outside, the storm howled with renewed vigor, strong enough to make the cabin creak. The sound of ice hitting the windowpanes became a nearly constant rattle.

"I'm glad I don't have to be out in this," Melinda said.

"I'm sure even the wild animals would agree with you. It's wicked."

"If it keeps up, I may have to turn on the generator. The stove might not be enough to keep the whole cabin warm."

"We could always just stay in this room. It's warm enough here."

"I guess it is." But she hadn't tried to sleep in a room with a man since…back then. And she wasn't sure she could do it. But it was still early, and things could change, so she forced the concern from her mind.

"I haven't had breakfast yet," she said, needing to move about and do something. "Are you hungry?"

"As a matter of fact, I am. Can I help?"

"I'll let you know."

As she passed by the radio, she switched it on in case Larry should call. She didn't want him worrying needlessly, because he was just the type to come out in this mess to check on her.

All she needed to make breakfast was a skillet and an old-fashioned toaster that held slices of bread at an angle over the hot stove top. Easier, she sometimes thought, than cooking on a regular stove.

Bacon was soon sizzling in the fry pan, and the aroma quickly roused Noel from his somnolence. He perked up, sniffing at the air.

Jon spoke. "You don't even have to teach him about people food."

"He already knows," she agreed.

"Will you give him some?"

She shook her head, smiling. "I'm not sure it would be good for him. Besides, do I really want to create a monster?"

"Most people eventually give in." He laughed. "How tough are you?"

"I guess we'll find out."

Noel suffered the indignity of being placed on the floor while they ate. He seemed to accept it as proper, though, and did nothing but rest his head between his paws and look up at them with soulful eyes.

Afterward, Jon followed her to the kitchen and helped with the dishes.

"You have no electricity without running your generator," he remarked. "So how do you get water?"

"The park has a small water treatment plant. We get it from the reservoir up the mountain, and the pumps are run by propane. It was the only economical way to bring clean water to the campgrounds."

"Makes sense. I was just curious."

"It was a good question." She smiled. "Most people don't even think to ask."

"So there's no electricity anywhere in the park?"

"Oh sure, there's an RV campground with hookups on the other side. This area is just rustic is all."

"Something for everyone."

"That's the idea. Either that or they just wanted to limit costs."

He laughed, and she realized she enjoyed making him laugh. She liked the way his eyes crinkled at the corners, loved the deep-from-the-belly sound of it. In fact, she thought as she gave him a sidelong glance, there was very little, if anything, that she didn't find attractive about him.

Even more oddly, instead of feeling embarrassed or uncomfortable now that she'd told him what had happened to her, she felt even more comfortable with him.

But there was another feeling, something beyond comfort. It put butterflies in her stomach and gave her a strange ache in places she normally avoided thinking about. For the first time since her abduction, she actually wondered if it would feel good to have a man's hands on her.

A shudder should have passed through her at the thought, but it didn't. Was it possible she was having the feelings of a normal woman for the first time in forever?

Before she could drag her gaze from him, he caught her eye. For a heart-stopping moment she thought she saw a flicker of heat there, a response to what she was feeling.

But it was impossible for him to read her mind, and surely her face revealed nothing. The edge of fear began to slice into her, but just in time he looked away, as if nothing had happened.

She was safe with him, she reminded herself. He had certainly proved that he intended her no harm. If anything, she suddenly realized with another burst of butterflies, she suspected that he was wondering if he was safe with her.

The thought gave her pause, and she stood motionless for a while, looking out at the whirling snow that had turned the trees into distant gray shadows. Could he be as uneasy about her as she was about him? Perhaps more so?

It didn't seem possible. And yet she couldn't escape the feeling.

The radio crackled then, and Larry's voice came across the airwaves, broken but audible.

"You there, Mel? Over."

Ignoring Jon, she hurried to the front room and reached for the microphone. "Hi, Larry, I'm here."

"I thought you'd want to know, this storm is still building. The word I'm getting is that we can expect to be pretty much snowed in for the next two days, if not a bit longer. Are you okay?"

"I've got everything I need, Larry."

"Same here. So we'll just ride it out, Mel." His laugh crackled over the speaker. "The only thing I'm worried about is all the avalanche danger we're going to have, and all the idiots who are going to want to get out on that fresh snow anyway."

"Yeah, but that's a few days away. I've already marked off a few areas."

"Same here. Maybe we'll have to close the park until we can take care of it."

"I was thinking about that. Might be wise, considering all the people who like to get off the trails."

"I'll see if I can clear it. Give me a call if you need anything, kiddo."

"Thanks, Larry. Out."

Jon was sitting on the couch again, Noel curled on his lap. "Your boss?"

"Chief ranger," she said, and nodded. "Just the two of us full-time. Usually it's enough."

"So people really are stupid enough to go off-trail on fresh snow?"

"Of course." She lifted a brow. "*You* ought to know how stupid people can be. And over the past few years, getting off the trails has been becoming more and more popular. It's beautiful out there, so I can understand the desire. Pristine. But the danger isn't worth it. Especially now, when we're getting fresh snow on top of a layer that probably crusted under the sun yesterday. The chance of the top layer slipping is huge."

He nodded, absently stroking Noel's head.

She turned the radio off once again to save the battery, then joined Jon and the dog on the couch. Noel lifted his head, stretched, then inched his way over so that he was squarely between them, as if claiming them both.

Melinda stroked one of his silky ears, watching his eyes grow heavy. There seemed to be a growing heaviness within her, as well. One that was making her more and more aware of the man nearby.

Her defenses dropped far enough that she noticed he smelled good. She hadn't allowed herself to pay attention to such a thing in years. He smelled *good*. In a way, that surprised her, since the sour smell of her abductor seemed to have shut down all her awareness of men in any respect except as threats.

God, was she going nuts? Yes, she'd known Jon, sort of, back when they were kids, but he'd been gone a long time and had come back a stranger. A couple of days of knowing him wasn't enough that she should be feeling like this. The risk was incalculable.

Nervous and unnerved, she jumped up from the couch. "Did I tell you about the bank robber?"

Chapter 8

Much later, the tension had fled the room. They had put up the Christmas tree and, after Melinda went out back and started the generator, spent some time admiring the fiber-optic lights as they changed color.

"It's almost pretty enough just like that," Jon remarked.

"I think so, too, but after a few days it starts to look bare. So I got some other stuff. Besides, I'll have the generator off more than on."

He nodded agreement, and helped take ornaments from their boxes and hang them by hooks on the limbs.

"I went for rustic stuff," she said. "I wanted it all

to look handmade or old. But sometimes I get a hankering for shiny balls, I have to admit."

"I think these ornaments are prettier. I ought to send you some things from Afghanistan. I think you'd like them."

"Handcrafts?"

"Yup." He smiled. "By and large, if they can't make it, they don't have it, so they've become amazingly adept at making toys for their children that are just fantastic. Some of the women have found markets outside the country for the things they make. Anything they can trade over the border in Pakistan, they do."

She paused with an ornament in her hand. "What are they like, the people?"

"Like people everywhere. Although I have to give them credit—they're cheerful in circumstances most of us in this country couldn't tolerate. I guess it's all in what you learn to expect as you grow up."

"It must be."

He placed a wooden sled on a bough and reached for another ornament. "Entire families sometimes load up mules and carry things over the mountains to sell. Women will spend all winter weaving with dyed wools, then go to cities to sell clothing and blankets. There's an organization that has been trying to help women build home businesses, then provide a way for them to sell on the international market. It's making progress, little by little, and where it has, the standard of living is improving."

"That's excellent."

"I think so."

They stopped to admire the tree when it was finished, then Jon made them some hot chocolate on the woodstove. The wind howled outside, and the snow blew wildly, but inside, all was safe and warm.

Noel needed a walk, and Jon insisted on taking him. Melinda stood at the front window and watched the man and pup walk out into the whipping snow. Noel, as usual, seemed to think the blizzard had been created for his pleasure. Jon just appeared impervious, standing so that his back faced the wind.

He let Noel pounce and prance with sheer delight in life until the pup began to tire. Then Jon tucked him up beneath one strong arm and brought him back inside.

The cold came in with them, a delicious contrast to the warmth indoors. Jon sucked the heat out of the air around him as if he were a black hole, even after he removed his jacket. "It's damn cold out there," he said.

He stepped toward the stove, aiming his backside at it, and nudged Noel a little to one side with, "Hey, *you* have a fur coat."

The pup cocked his head, then settled a little farther away on the hearthstones, happily licking the remaining snow from his coat.

Melinda went to the other window to look out at the large round thermometer. She had hung it on a tree where it was reasonably well protected from wind and sun. "My God, Jon, it's thirty-two below out there. Out of the wind. You'd better let me go out next time. I've got the gear for this."

"Or we could just train His Highness here to use a litter box."

Melinda giggled. "That would really confuse him, don't you think?"

Jon grinned. "He's already confused. He thinks this storm is fun."

"It is. As long as we don't have to go out in it."

"He kinda makes that point moot, don't you think?"

His eyes were sparkling, lively, inviting. So different from the way he had looked when she'd first seen him at Mahoney's. He'd shed the so-called thousand-yard stare and was truly in the here and now.

And that made him so attractive she ached. Frightened by her own feelings, she started to turn away, but he stopped her. His grip on her arm was gentle, nonthreatening. Hands that could kill touched her as kindly as a lover. Slowly, she looked at him again.

"You feel it, too," he said huskily.

She studied his face, trying to read his meaning, while her heart hammered in her chest. "Feel what?" she stalled, although she was pretty sure she knew what he meant.

"This…thing pulling us together. It's been there ever since you walked up to me at the bar." He nodded, as if feeling the rightness of his own words. "You felt it then. You wouldn't have spoken to me otherwise."

She couldn't deny it. Their meeting had been entirely out of character for her. Sometimes when she went into town she stopped at Mahoney's for a drink. Always one drink. Always a draft. And never, ever, did she speak to anyone except Mahoney himself or one of the deputies she knew. She certainly never approached anyone.

Slowly she nodded. Her heart was beating so hard now that she could hardly breathe.

"I wouldn't have talked to you, or gone to the diner with you, if I hadn't felt the same pull."

Now she held her breath, as if the day had suddenly been transformed into finely spun crystal that might break at a whisper.

"I came home because I had to come home," he continued, his voice huskier and quieter still. The wind outside seemed louder. "And I'm going back because I have to go back. I have to take care of my men."

She nodded, just a tiny movement.

"But…" He inched closer. "I want you."

He dropped his hand from her arm, as if to let her know she was free, completely free, to decide however she wished. But the instant his touch was gone, she missed it. A whole tide of feelings rushed in, things she hadn't been allowing herself to think about, things she had put away for years, things she had refused to acknowledge in herself since she saw Jon at Mahoney's.

All those things were there, vibrant and alive, but hidden behind fear.

She couldn't speak now. Her heart was in her throat, and she felt as if she were paralyzed in a moment of expectation so heavy it filled her every cell. She wanted him. It had been so long since she had felt any such thing. It had been so long since she had been near a man other than Nate Tate without feeling at least a frisson of fear.

She wanted to raise her hand and reach for him. Wanted him to reach out and gather her close. But she couldn't move. Couldn't stir. A web of past and present wrapped her and confined her.

He gave a small nod and started to turn away. It was that movement that set her free.

"Jon," she said hoarsely.

He looked at her again and apparently saw all he needed to know. He reached out with his powerful arms and gathered her to his chest, holding her. Just holding her. Snugly. Making a safe place for her within his strength.

Something let go, a terror so old it had become part of the very fabric of her soul. The instant it eased, she felt utter relaxation fill her, and with it came new seeds of confidence.

"You're a brave woman," he said softly, still holding her snugly, yet not moving. His breath stirred her hair, its warmth welcome. "Not many people could have done what you did to survive. Not many *would* have survived."

Lots of people had said that to her after she was rescued, but this was the first time she believed it. Maybe because it came from someone who had survived his own ordeal: war. Someone who was willing to face it again.

If he could be so brave, why couldn't she?

Slowly she lifted her arms and hugged him back, certain that nothing in her life had ever felt so right. She was able to melt against him and revel in the splendor of the moment. In the warmth of human contact, something she hadn't known since her parents had died.

But this was even stronger, elemental in a different way. Almost by instinct, she rubbed her cheek against his flannel shirt, loving its softness even as she loved the hardness of his chest beneath. Hard, soft, exquisite beyond words.

Then she tilted her head up and looked deep into his eyes.

And knew that, for this moment at least, everything was all right.

Chapter 9

The thick curtains in her bedroom were drawn to keep warmth in. The heat from the woodstove still reached the back of the house, but the wind blowing across the glass sucked it out rapidly.

In the darkness, they moved hesitantly, both filled with caution. It was as if they both sensed they were about to cross a dangerous barrier and had better be very careful about how they did it. The hunger and need were tamped down for now, giving way to gentleness and concern.

The thought flitted across Melinda's mind that they were like two wounded animals approaching cautiously, then dancing away on the strange, welcome sparkle of being wanted.

They lay side by side on the bed and embraced, fully clothed. The safety net was still in place. In an instant, either of them could pull back from the precipice.

But the warmth of holding and being held began to thaw the frozen places in both of them. Slowly, surely, they relaxed more and more into one another.

When Melinda felt soft from head to toe, languorous in a way she couldn't remember ever feeling, he moved his hand and began to stroke her hair gently. It felt so good that she instinctively murmured and pressed even closer.

But he didn't take that as an invitation to rush ahead. Instead he kept stroking her hair, occasionally drawing his hand down her back, which only made her feel better and more relaxed.

Time had lost meaning for them. They had all the time in the world, or so it seemed. And it felt so right.

Surprise filled Melinda as she realized she was smiling into his chest. This was something she had never believed would be possible, to feel this comfortable and good with a man again. Raising her arms, she looped them around his neck, just enjoying being held by someone who wanted to hold her.

But of course they could not stay suspended there forever. They had come here because of a deep and basic need. If Melinda had allowed herself to think about what to do, she probably would have panicked.

He didn't give her the option. His hand slid down her back, then up under her shirt, and oh, it felt so good. His hand was warm, rough with calluses, gentle and slow, asking for nothing more, demanding nothing.

His touch nearly hypnotized her. She began to feel as if she would sink into the mattress. Into him. And that was exactly where she wanted to be.

When he unclasped her bra and she felt her breasts fall free, she sucked in air with astonishment. He froze, but she had just passed the point of her last inhibition, or so it seemed at that moment, because she squirmed closer and whispered, "Oh, Jon…Jon…"

He let go the whisper of a sigh, as if he had been holding his breath, then cupped her breast in his warm hand.

Instantly electric sensations she had never imagined darted along her nerve endings, directly to her center, making her feel heavy and hungry all at once. A small moan escaped her as his thumb found her hardening nipple and began to brush it to even greater excitement.

Too much…too much… Needs and hungers ignored for a decade swamped her, causing her to writhe against him, lifting her higher and higher. Her hips began to move almost desperately as a tightening ache pulled her closer and closer and…

The most amazing thing happened. One instant she was climbing, unsure if she would reach the crest, and the next she exploded into a cataclysm of release.

As if he knew it, he slipped his thigh up between her legs and pressed his hand to her bottom, pulling her tight and close, encouraging her to ride the rhythmic waves of satisfaction.

Slowly her paroxysms eased. She felt exhausted, wonderful and, for an instant, embarrassed. "I'm sorry," she whispered. She had acted like an animal, with no thought for him.

"Don't ever be sorry for that," he murmured roughly. "Never, ever."

"But—"

He covered her lips with a finger. "Shh," he said gently. "You'll see."

He held her tightly and stroked her back, sprinkling the occasional kiss on her face until she once again relaxed. Then his hand renewed its journey, finding her breast, reawakening the electric sparkles that danced through her. Somehow the shirt vanished and her bra with it, and he lowered his head, taking her nipple into his mouth.

An exclamation escaped her as the novel sensation restoked her hunger and filled her with amazement. He sucked hard, then gently, then nibbled a little and catapulted her back to the heights.

Impatience filled her, and this time she was determined not to take the trip alone.

She pulled at the buttons of his shirt. A little laugh escaped him, a pleased sound, and he drew away long enough to help her.

Then came the magic of skin on skin, her breasts to his muscled chest, soft to hard, exquisite beyond description. Sinuously as a cat, she twisted against him, wanting whatever came next, but unsure where they were heading.

He moved a little and pressed her face to his chest, guiding her, until she took his small nipple in her mouth and mimicked what he had done to her. The groan that escaped him gave her a feeling of power and pleasure, a heady combination that encouraged her to want more, to do more.

When he pulled at her sweatpants, she was more than ready to wiggle out of both them and her panties. Then she reached for the snap of his jeans, wanting to remove the last barrier.

He obliged swiftly, sending clothes flying across the room. Then they came together with nothing between them any longer and she felt the hardness of him pressed to her abdomen. The sensation both astonished her and made everything within her sizzle.

She couldn't seem to breathe. There wasn't enough air in the room. Her heart thudded heavily as she began to move her hands over him, wanting to know every inch of him, wanting to discover his every mystery.

He groaned at her touch. Occasionally she felt a scar and her heart skipped a beat, but she didn't stop. That was for later. For now there were only these moments in Eden while she discovered what it meant to be a woman.

It meant power and joy and a sense of fierce protectiveness, and a hunger that knew no bounds. She pulled back just a little to drink him in with her eyes in the dim light.

Before she could do much more than scan him, he took her breath away by the simple expedient of slipping his hand between her legs.

For an instant she clamped her legs around him; then a delicious weakness filled her, and she parted her legs, offering herself to him.

His fingers were wicked, finding the most sensitive knot of nerves. A cry escaped her, and she tried to press herself harder against his hand. He teased her to near madness.

All of a sudden, without conscious thought, she rose over him and straddled him. She looked down at his face, finding his eyes closed but his lips parted in a faint smile.

Then he was entering her. Never had she felt anything like that before. There was an instant of sharp pain, but it was gone before she could do anything except gasp. Then she enveloped him and knew that she had been born for this moment, these sensations.

Gently he drew her down on his chest, so that they were close. Their bodies were slick, and this new position minimized their movements in the most tantalizing way.

Just a little, just a little…

"Oh, Mel," she heard him whisper hoarsely. "Oh, Mel…"

The sound of his voice thrilled her. Everything thrilled her, and then her body took over, carrying her to places where thought had no meaning.

She heard him cry out sharply, then heard her own keening as she tumbled once more over that magical, wonderful precipice of climax.

Nothing could be more beautiful.

Chapter 10

Something tickled her leg. She moved, not wanting to wake up from the delicious half sleep that held her in thrall. She thought she had known peace in her life, but this was beyond her wildest dreams. She didn't want to move until the world ended.

The tickle came again, and suddenly Jon's laugh rumbled into her ear through his chest wall.

"What?" she asked drowsily, collapsed on him as if he were the best bed in the world.

"We have a visitor."

She turned her head, peeling her eyelids open a bit, and saw a certain white and gray husky standing on his hind legs nosing at them. It had been his nuzzling she had felt.

Jon patted the bed, and the dog jumped up. He had his own ideas about the proper protocol for these moments, and before either of them could move, an eager little tongue was lapping at their arms and faces. Jon burst out laughing and rolled carefully, depositing Melinda on the bed beside him. Then he reached for the pup with one hand and brought the dog to lie between them.

Noel seemed to think that was good, because at once he curled into a tight little ball and closed his eyes.

"That," Jon said, "was not exactly my idea of a romantic moment."

Melinda looked at him, a smile tugging at the corners of her mouth. "No?"

"Little imp." He looked from the dog to her, then touched her cheek. "No," he said. "This is where I want to tell you just how beautiful you are. What a wonderful lover you are."

The blush that had never managed to emerge before now suffused her face. She could feel its heat and was grateful the room was dim. "Thank you."

He smiled and pulled the coverlet up over them, then held her as close as he could with the dog between them. Surprisingly, Noel remained right where he was, undisturbed by being completely covered.

Slowly they drifted off to sleep. Outside, the raging world began to quiet.

For now at least.

A soft tongue licking her cheek awoke Melinda sometime in the afternoon. She opened her eyes and looked straight into Noel's beautiful blue ones. When he saw her eyes open, he hopped to his feet, and cold air rushed under the blanket.

"Cruel," she said to him. "That was cruel."

He simply took another swipe at her with his tongue. A giggle escape her, and she pushed him gently away, realizing she was alone in the bed.

Her heart stopped; then a wave of panic set in. Had Jon left her? After all, why should he stay? She could hear that the wind had settled down, and now that they'd had sex, maybe he wanted nothing more to do with her.

But before she could completely freak, she heard the sound of his voice from elsewhere in the cabin. He was singing "God Rest Ye Merry, Gentlemen" in a pleasant baritone, punctuated by clattering from the kitchen.

Panic turned into a smile, and she clambered out of bed, reaching for the warmest clothes she could find.

The kitchen was warmer than the bedroom, but Jon was nowhere in sight. She found him in the front room, cooking something on the stove that smelled absolutely delicious, perking a pot of coffee and putting up a garland over the door.

He saw her and grinned. "I hope that's where you wanted this."

"It's perfect."

Warmth filled her from the top of her head down to her toes, which were stuffed into thick socks. She wiggled them happily and settled on the couch. "It was getting cold back there."

"I noticed. That's why I got up. The heat drew me like a moth to a flame." He tapped in a small nail and draped the artificial garland over it. "I hope I didn't leave you freezing."

"I wasn't that cold until I got out of bed."

"Part of it was the fire was burning low, but if you look out, you'll see the thermometer has some interesting news."

Curious, she went to the window. "Forty below?" Astonishment made her look a second time. "That's not real."

"Unfortunately, it is. I turned on the radio, and your friend Larry called a little while ago to warn you not even to walk the dog."

She looked at Noel, who was nosing at the lower limbs of the Christmas tree as if he liked watching the ornaments swing. "What are we going to do about that?"

"He and I came to an agreement. I let him use paper in the bathroom and cleaned it up."

"Oh." She experienced an irrational spurt of resentment at the way he seemed to be taking over, then dismissed it. *This,* she told herself, *is what comes from living like a hermit for so long.* Inability to make room for another person.

The thought depressed her, and she folded her arms as she returned to her seat on the couch. She ought to be enjoying this rare time of hominess. She'd had little enough of it since...*then.*

"Are you all right?" he asked.

Startled from her thoughts, she looked at him. "Sure. Just...ghosts, I guess."

He nodded and draped the garland over one last nail. "We all have them. Some more than others."

"Do you have a lot of them?"

"What do you think?" His smile became crooked. "I've got them by the bucketload."

"That must be terrible."

He shrugged. "There's a price for everything. Sometimes it's pretty high."

She bit her lower lip then blurted, "How do you stay sane?"

He froze for a good fifteen seconds. Then he came to sit on the couch, looking away from her. "Sometimes I'm not sure I am. Sometimes I'm not sure I want to be. Over there...well, you have to lop off parts of yourself. Not feel things. It's necessary. The question is whether I'll get those parts back once I'm done."

She nodded, resisting the urge to take his hand. "Do you think you will?"

He looked at her then. "I think I already have."

The words pierced her, causing her to release something that was nearly a sob. "Me too," she said, then crawled down the couch until she could climb into his arms. "Me too."

The tears began rolling down her face but she didn't wipe them away.

It was, in some sense, almost like being reborn. And it hurt every bit as much.

Later they ate stew, snuggling together before the fire. Then, as if pulled by the same need, they returned to the bedroom. Noel wanted to take his place on the bed, but they persuaded him to stay off as they indulged again in the wonders of lovemaking.

Melinda grew increasingly convinced that life had never been so beautiful.

Later, as night claimed the world and the storm rebuilt beyond the walls, they remained snuggled naked together in the bed, offering gentle touches, laughing when Noel burrowed into the blankets, then tossed them with his nose as if they were snow.

They talked, building bridges, about little things that would interest no one else. About childhood memories, about parents and friends, about hopes and dreams.

It was the latter subject that finally brought some sobriety, as they realized their dreams were few.

"That's sad," Melinda finally said. "We ought to

have some hopes for the future that don't involve everything staying the same forever."

"I know. Maybe you want to be a chief ranger yourself?"

"The odd thing is that I haven't even thought about it. I've been like a mole contentedly buried in my little hole here. I guess I ran away from everything. Very different from you."

"Not really. I ran into something, I guess. Always wanted to be in Special Ops. But once I got there, I discovered I had to start running from everything else. Everything that could soften me in any way."

She nodded, her head resting on his shoulder so he could feel it. "I can identify with that."

"There are all kinds of walls you have to build."

"For self-protection," she said.

"Exactly. I guess we tore a few of them down."

"We did," she agreed. "And I'm not sorry. I just think it's sad that neither of us is looking for anything different or special tomorrow."

He turned onto his side, drawing her close. "I just found something special, and I don't want to let it go."

She drew a sharp breath and tilted her head, trying to read his face by the light of the oil lamp.

His expression was totally serious. "I'm not asking anything right now except that you think about this, okay? No pressure. It's too early to answer anyway."

Her heart slammed. "What?"

"I think I'm falling in love with you." He pressed his finger to her lips before she could say anything. "Don't answer. We haven't known each other long enough to be sure of it. Either of us. But I know where my feelings are headed. I just want you to think about it. I'll think about it, too. Let's nurture what we've started and see where it goes. That's all I'm asking."

"Okay," she breathed around his finger. "Okay."

"I mean, I have to go back to Afghanistan, again. Just once more. That's not something you want to commit to unless you're very, very sure. So…just think about it. About your own feelings, okay?"

She nodded. "I will. I promise. I'm starting to feel—"

"Shh. Don't say it, Mel. It's way too soon. Way too soon."

"Okay." Then she closed her eyes and wiggled even closer. If these few days were all she had, she wanted every single moment of them.

Because this was the best thing life had ever brought her.

Chapter 11

Christmas Eve morning finally arrived a week later, dawning with a crystalline blue sky bright enough to bring tears to the eyes.

Noel started the day with howling and frantic dancing by the door. Jon and Melinda both immediately pulled on their cold weather gear. They did everything together now, even walking the dog.

But as Melinda reached for her sunglasses, she realized there was something different about Noel's behavior. She reached out swiftly and touched Jon's arm.

"What?" he asked.

"Something's wrong."

"Why do you say—" But before he finished the sentence, there was a thud against the side of the cabin, as if something had fallen into it. Noel's frenzy built.

"What's out there?" Jon asked.

"My truck and snowmobile."

"Stay here."

"No way."

Their eyes met and spoke silently. They were both thinking about the escaped bank robber.

"I have a gun," Melinda said.

"Get it. But I'm going out first."

"He's *armed*."

"That's nothing new. I'll go around to the right, you circle from the left with the gun."

"Okay." The agreement was hard to make, but she understand what he wanted, and why.

When she went to get the gun, she put Noel in the bathroom, and closed the door against his howls and his puppy growls.

They opened the cabin door as silently as possible. Jon waited until Melinda had disappeared around the other side of the cabin, then began to walk toward the lean-to carport, allowing his booted feet to crunch on the snow. The last thing he wanted to do was to startle the guy. This time he didn't think silence would be his friend.

As he rounded the corner of the cabin, the first things he noted were the silence and emptiness. No other person was in sight, but in the same instant he saw that the snowmobile had been moved. The tracks behind it were as fresh as yesterday's snow.

Someone had been trying to steal it. A quick survey told him where the best hiding places were, and an instant of evaluation indicated which one would be smartest.

In that instant he leapt into action with the speed that had saved his life on more than one occasion.

At a run he jumped on the hood of the SUV, crouched as he crossed its roof, then jumped downward on a startled man.

He knocked the guy back on the snow, but it didn't end there. A gun appeared in the robber's hand, and they wrestled for it, rolling in the snow, each man trying to get the upper hand. Jon held the guy's wrist in a vicelike grip, knowing that whatever else occurred, he couldn't allow the man to take air.

Jon grunted as a knee caught him in the stomach, but the pain only seemed to make him stronger. "Drop it," he said to the robber. "Drop it or I'll kill you."

Another twist and he had his other arm right across the guy's throat, pressing hard until the gunman's eyes began to bulge.

"Drop it!" Melinda's voice came from the back end of the carport. "I've got a gun, and I'll blow your head off."

Her voice was as smooth and cold as ice. She meant it.

Slowly, eyes still bulging, the man dropped his

pistol into the snow. Freed of that threat, Jon moved swiftly, turning the man over, holding him down with a knee to his back and his wrists pinned.

Then he spoke, breathing heavily. "Get the gun, Mel. Get the gun. Then go radio Nate. I think we've got his bank robber."

Without a word, Mel grabbed up the gun and ran for the radio inside.

"I didn't rob any bank," the guy said. "Man, my cheek is freezing!"

"It's going to keep freezing until the sheriff gets here. And we'll let *him* decide what to do with you."

Melinda returned five minutes later with some rope. "Nate's on his way. You want to tie him up?"

Jon looked up at her and grinned when he saw she was still armed. "Yeah. It's a helluva Christmas present, huh?"

At that Mel laughed, reacting to the adrenaline rush. "One helluva present. Especially for the teller he shot."

Chapter 12

Christmas Eve itself arrived with light snow, picture-perfect flakes that could have adorned a postcard. Tomorrow they would go to the Tates' and share dinner with that big, bustling family, but tonight was quiet and their own.

The tree glowed brightly, lit up by the generator, but otherwise they continued to rely on oil lamps and the orange gleam of the stove. Christmas carols played on Melinda's battery-operated player, carols she had chosen for their quietness and mood. "Silent Night" never failed to fill her with a wonderful sense of peace.

Jon had wedged himself into a corner of the couch, and Melinda lifted her legs onto the cushions and leaned back against his chest. He kept his arm around her shoulders, just under her chin.

Noel, happy and sleepy after a Christmas meal of liver mixed with dog food, had chosen his favorite spot near the stove to sleep.

"I have a gift for you," Jon murmured as the strains of "Silent Night" gave way to a choral version of "The First Noel." "I hope you don't mind."

"Why would I mind?" But that reminded her of the gift she had for him, one she was uneasy about, because in a way it seemed so presumptuous. It also wasn't very much, but she didn't know what he could possibly take back to Afghanistan with him.

"You never know," he answered. "Let me get it."

"No," she said. "Mine first."

He laughed. "Okay, then."

She climbed off the couch and went to the tree. There were packages for Noel, too. When she and Jon had gone to town a few days ago, they'd both had the same thought: rawhide bones and a few squeaky toys for the dog. But those could wait.

First she handed him an unwrapped tin of butter cookies. "You mentioned always liking these. Maybe you can eat them on your way back."

"This is so nice," he said, and there was no mistaking his honesty. "It's been a long time." He didn't wait but opened the tin and popped a cookie into his mouth. A smile creased the corners of his eyes as he gave her a thumbs-up.

Her heart was beating more rapidly now, so she waited a few seconds before finally reaching for the red envelope on the tree. She had intentionally avoided putting his name on it, so he wouldn't guess it was for him.

He accepted it, a question in his eyes. He tore the flap open carefully and pulled out a card that said something mushy. "This so nice…." His voice trailed off as he opened the card and something slipped out.

He picked it up slowly, looking at it. It was a laminated pocket photo of Melinda.

She waited, but he just kept staring at it. She cleared her throat finally. "I thought the lamination would help protect it over…over there."

"It will," he said huskily. "God, you're beautiful. I can hardly wait to show you off."

Her cheeks heated. "I didn't know what else you could take with you…."

His gaze caught hers. "Quit trying to apologize. This is exactly what I wanted. I just didn't know how to ask for it. Thank you. This means the world."

She relaxed then, for there could be no doubting his sincerity. He stared at the photo a little longer, then slipped it in his breast pocket. "I'll always keep it right here, by my heart."

He held out his arms, and she crawled back into them, her face against his chest, feeling happy, so happy.

"Thank you," he said again, and kissed her.

They were distracted only by the sound of Noel yawning and scratching himself. Slowly they pulled apart, gazing deeply into each other's eyes.

"Now it's my turn," Jon said. His eyes almost seemed to dance, but she could sense nervousness there, too. The way she had been feeling.

He moved her gently to the side and went to his jacket. He stuck his hand in the pocket and removed a small box with a ribbon on it. She caught her breath, because things that came in boxes like that were generally a lot more expensive than a laminated photo.

He sat beside her, the beribboned box in his hands. "This is something I want you to have, regardless of what you may decide about us with time."

"What do you mean?"

"I told you I was falling in love with you but we needed time to be sure."

"I remember."

"I'm pretty sure, but maybe you aren't." He tried to smile but looked strained, as if he were worried. Slowly, almost reluctantly, he lifted the lid from the box, and revealed a ruby and diamond ring.

"Oh my!" she gasped.

"You can take this as a friendship ring if you want," he said quickly. "Or…or as something more. Because I'm sure how I feel about *you*, Melinda. I'm in love with you. I want to come home to you. But I realize you might not feel the same. So just wear this because we're friends."

Before she could speak, he slipped it onto the ring finger of her right hand.

She held it up, looking at it, then looking at him. "Jon, I… I don't know what to say. This is so beautiful! I've never been given anything so precious."

"You don't have to say anything," he said quickly. "Just enjoy it."

"How could I not enjoy it? But there's something you need to know."

He nodded, growing solemn. "And that is?"

"You forgot to look at the back of the picture I gave you."

His brow knitted, then he reached into his pocket, bringing out the photo and turning it over.

Slowly his face relaxed and a grin began to spread from ear to ear.

"You love me," he said.

"Absolutely," she agreed. Then she pulled the ring from her right hand and put it on her left.

He threw back his head and laughed, waking Noel, who immediately jumped up between them, his tail wagging. It was his own fault he got squeezed between them when they embraced.

"I didn't dare hope," he said.

"Me either."

"It won't be easy."

"No, but I'm patient," she answered. "I'm happy here, and until you're finished over there, well, that's just how it will have to be."

Noel squeaked and wiggled out from between them. Neither of them noticed.

Jon raised a hand to her hair, touching her as if he couldn't believe his senses.

"For now," Melinda said seriously, "this is probably the best way for both of us. I don't know that I'm ready yet for a normal life."

"Me neither," he admitted. "When I come home, I don't know how fast I'll get myself back together."

"We'll work on it together," she promised him. "That's what we do for people we love."

He pulled her close again, burying his face in her shoulder. "You're the best Christmas present in the world, Mel. The best. I love you so much!"

"I love you, too." She clung to him, happy, so happy, for the first time in memory. She could face the long lonely days with the memory of right now.

A sharp bark pulled them apart. Noel stood by the door, tail wagging, gaze demanding.

"You know," Jon said, "he has amazing timing."

"He sure does." But as she watched Jon pull on his jacket and pick up the leash, she suddenly realized something. In his own way, Noel had helped bring them together by lowering their first line of defense. Smiling so broadly that her cheeks hurt, she watched the dog prance as Jon began to open the door.

"You're the best, Noel," she said quietly.

Jon looked at her with an arched brow.

She added hastily, "Second to you, of course."

They were both laughing as he and the dog stepped out into the magic of Christmas Eve.

* * * * *

CHRISTMAS AT HIS COMMAND
Catherine Mann

To my children, my miracles. Thank you for making every Christmas come alive with your joy and wonder, no matter how old you grow!

Acknowledgments

I had an absolute blast traveling to another country (in my mind!) for Christmas with this novella. While I've had the pleasure of visiting Germany, my trip there came during the summer months, so I owe a huge debt of gratitude to my friends overseas for sharing their holiday experiences with me.

To my dear pal in Germany, Kris Alice Hohls, thank you for the delightful tales of Christmas in your home. And many thanks as well for those awesome sugar cookies back in Denver! You rock!

To my newfound friend in Bavaria, Christine Spoel. Thank you for the enjoyable times we had while you and your charming family lived in the States. I delight in our continued friendship—as well as the fun Christmas packages you send each year generously loaded with local holiday delicacies!

To my longtime air force buddy, Katherine Dunn. Thank you, thank you, treasured friend for detailing your experiences from being stationed in Germany and spending Christmas in Bavaria. We've shared so many travels over our near twenty years of knowing each other. I just wish we could have walked together along those holiday vendor stalls you so beautifully described! Oh, the damage we could have done to our credit cards!!

Merry Christmas! *Fröhliche Weihnachten!*

Chapter 1

General Hank Renshaw hadn't often seen a man's hand down the bra of esteemed senator, Ginger Landis.

Of course, as he stood astounded in the doorway of the VIP lounge in the tiny airport on the Bavarian border, he couldn't recall a time he'd ever seen his longtime friend Ginger's underwear at all. Much less with a man's hand slipped inside.

Hank slammed the door closed so nobody else would snag a view of what now filled his eyes.

Technically, the security fellow wasn't groping around inside her satiny camisole thing. Ginger had taken off the jacket to her Christmas-red power suit so the reedy guy in a black coat could outfit her with the latest listening device for her upcoming meeting with the German Chancellor and Minister of Arts as well as the Vice-Chancellor of neighboring Kasov. All a part of a holiday goodwill trip across Europe, ending on Christmas Eve at a medieval castle with chapel ruins set to be rebuilt. Ginger would be donating an heirloom from her family's antique art collection, a small but priceless porcelain crèche.

Hank's role? To stand at her side as her official military escort. Unofficially, he was here to protect her. He was the final wall of defense between her and the threats that had been made on her life. Those threats were the very reason for the heightened security with a listening device.

Arms extended, Ginger stood in spike heels, legs to kill in a pencil-thin skirt and satin camisole trimmed in lace.

His midnight dreams about this woman played out much like this—with *him* standing beside her, of course. He would stretch her out on that froufrou creamy chaise behind her.

But only in dreams when he tossed off the restraints of waking hours did he allow himself to fall victim to fantasies about his pal of over twenty-five years. He was a red-blooded man, after all, and age hadn't diminished Ginger's appeal in the least. Which could also have something to do with the genius brain she packed underneath that head of perfectly styled platinum-blond hair.

Still, never had he done anything to put their friendship at risk by relaying the attraction.

Then he realized the silence had gone on too long to be anything but freaking awkward, and his slack-jawed look could very well put a chink in their all-important friendship.

"Sorry, Senator Landis." Hank used her official title in deference to the security personnel present—and out of a need to put some distance back into their relationship. "I hadn't realized you weren't ready yet. I'll just step outside."

Outside. A fine place for him to stand guard anyway, while he sweated his way through images of her wearing red-hot lingerie. This would be a very long day.

He twisted the doorknob behind him.

Ginger waved a manicured hand through the air, white tips of her nails fluttering. "Oh, hell, Hank. Quit with all that formal madame stuff. We're not at a press conference."

She had a point. Still he couldn't help thinking he would be safer standing guard in the airport corridor by the decorated tree getting his head on straight again. "Ginger, I'll wait in the hall by the door until you're ready."

"Hold on. Get out from under that mistletoe and come over here. See if you can clip this microphone on right so I'm not trailing tiny computer bits out of my skirt," her South Carolina drawl curled through the cloud of unease. "This poor secret service fellow's so worried about copping a feel he can't get the damn thing secured to save his soul."

The young security agent must have been all of seventeen—okay, twenty-seven. They just looked like babies when you'd hit fifty-five.

The kid didn't help matters by blushing to the roots of his Idaho-farm-boy red hair. "Senator Landis, I apologize. These new listening devices have a tricky clasp, but they're far less visible."

Ginger cocked a delicately arched brow. "Well, I wanted to use those fancy teeny-tiny ones that fit in the ear canal, but all this flying gave me a double ear infection."

She smoothed a hand over her blond hair away from the aforementioned ailing ears. The simple gesture hitched her camisole up to expose a tiny strip of stomach when Hank was already reeling from the surprise of seeing his old friend in a new light. Hank blinked his way through the fog and focused on her words. She'd mentioned being sick? Concern slammed away everything else.

He charged deeper into the room, the plush carpet muting his frustrated footsteps to dull thuds. "Are you sure you're up to this trip? They've packed in more stops on this goodwill tour than there are waking hours in the day."

"I'm fine. The antibiotic's kicked in. My ears are just a little sensitive."

Relief rocked through him as the secret service agent stepped away from her, giving Hank a clear path. Yeah, he knew he was a little overprotective of women. His daughters labeled him an alarmist when it came to illnesses. Send a bullet or mortar fire his way and he could stand firm without flinching. But ailments of the body still made him break out in a cold sweat since he'd lost his wife to a fluke aneurysm twenty-four years ago, leaving him with three children to bring up.

He didn't know how he would have made it through without Ginger's help. He'd tried to help her as well when her senator husband had died ten years ago in a car crash, leaving her with four strapping boys. She and Hank had pooled resources when they could.

He blinked through thoughts of the past, their past, their friendship. Anything to keep himself from focusing overlong on the fact that his fingers were now inches away from Ginger's chest.

Her breasts.

Hell. What was he thinking? She was an esteemed member of the Senate Arms Committee, for Pete's sake. He considered himself nonsexist, a professional. He'd risen through the ranks treating everyone in his command equally, fairly. So get the job done.

He slid his hand inside Ginger's camisole. He schooled his features to stay blank in spite of the fact that her creamy skin smoothed along the back of his hand with a sweet temptation reminding him how long it had been since he'd been with a woman.

There had been invitations, but his rank kept him from accepting most of them, and his jammed schedule eradicated most of the rest. He adjusted the clamp to a crevice in the lace. Damn it all, he wasn't some unseasoned kid to be floored by a simple stroke against skin.

But he *was* man enough to appreciate the subtler temptations of life as being far more seductive than blatant displays.

Sweet sin, something shifted in his world in that moment. It didn't matter that he was an old cantankerous bomber pilot, widowed father of three, a grandpa even. He couldn't make himself look away from the holly-green of Ginger's eyes.

She cocked her head to the side. "Hank?"

He whipped his hand free. "All set."

Hank tugged her jacket from the back of an ornate wooden chair and held the coat open for her to slide her arms inside. Then his brain tripped over itself.

Hell.

This wasn't an overcoat. It was *clothing*. He should have simply passed the jacket to her while waiting to give her the velvet bag that held the miniature porcelain crèche. Now, he couldn't miss the intimacy of helping her dress. Luckily, Ginger simply smoothed over the moment by taking it in her normal easy stride that had aided her in negotiating legislation during senatorial debates.

She slipped one slim arm then the other inside, shrugging the suit jacket into place. Her fingers glided down the golden buttons until she was once again fully clothed. "Thank you, Hank."

Too bad he still saw satin and lace.

Not wise. He needed to remember that he was here as part of Ginger's protective detail for this string of politically strategic visits across Europe. With two death threats and pockets of terrorist cells all over Eastern Europe, her security had to be his number-one priority.

His brain didn't have room for satin and lace when her life could be in danger. But because of those very problems with spreading terrorist factions, she'd stressed more than ever the need for strengthening ties between their country and representatives from countries on their list.

Ginger stepped forward, the hem of her sleeve gripped in her fist and reached to rub the fabric over his shoulders. "You've got snowflakes melting on your uniform. Don't want to tarnish those three shiny stars on your shoulder boards."

"Thanks, it's kicking up out there, but I'll have an umbrella to cover you on the way to the limo." He kept his face stern. "I'm going to state the obvious— *again*. You should wear a bulletproof vest."

"Impossible to hide under this suit." She shook her head.

"Easy enough to hide beneath your overcoat if we kept your appearances outside."

"We can only take security so far without insulting the people we're trying to win over." She tapped his temple as if the awkward moment had never happened. "What's done is done, so lighten up. What's wrong with you today, Hank?"

He let his real feelings show for the first time since he'd been frozen solid in the doorway. "I'm worried about you. I've got a bad feeling about this that I just can't shake. You're sick with that ear infection anyway. Why not bow out of the next two days of meetings and just make the final appearance at the chapel ruins?"

"Oh Hank, you know better. We've come a long way from when our kids used to play together while we drank a bottomless pitcher of tea with Benjamin and Jessica."

Benjamin and Jessica. Ginger's husband. His wife. Back when they'd all been friends and who'd thought of the future? "Or longneck bottles of beer."

"That too." Ginger gave his shoulders a final swipe and pat. "You gave up personal-comfort choices when you took on your position with the Joint Chiefs of Staff. And I'm taking a walk I never expected when Benjamin decided to get out of the Air Force and run for the Senate. So let's put on our best game face and do our jobs."

Their jobs. Right. Except as he stared down into her deep-green eyes and wondered why she wasn't as affected by the moment as he was, he realized her hands still rested on his shoulders.

Her hand resting in the crook of Hank's elbow, Ginger stepped out of the airport, her time to "freshen up" in the VIP lounge over. Her stomach clenched. From the security threats, surely. Not from the surprise jolt of awareness she felt from taking the arm of the towering man beside her. This was her longtime pal, her dear friend.

A man who had been *unmistakably* checking her out.

Her nerves fluttered like the trills of music from the band playing Christmas tunes under the red-striped awning. "Oh, Tannenbaum" floated on the snowy swirls as she made her way along the preswept red carpet leading to the limo fifty feet away.

Hank held the umbrella as she waved to the distant crowd who'd braved the snowstorm to welcome them. She had almost gotten to the point where she didn't notice the protective detail. However her safety depended on it, and she simply had to accept that.

Cameras flashed and snapped as reporters caught their images for the papers and the Internet. She strode past the cargo plane with its spit-polished crew who had hauled all their gear, personnel and vehicles across the Atlantic, then around Europe. The redheaded secret service agent walked alongside, talking into his sleeve.

Hank stayed ever-present in step, his strides a loose march, snow spiraling around their feet. She gripped his arm, her velvet bag dangling from her elbow. She wasn't sure why she'd been so insistent on carrying the crèche herself. It would have been simpler to include it with the luggage. But she'd always treasured the little piece, one of her children's Christmas favorites each year and she wanted to keep it with her as long as she could.

Hank's face dipped toward hers. "Is the microphone on yet?" His voice rumbled low.

"No, General, not until I'm in the meeting with the German Chancellor and the Vice-Chancellor of Kasov," she answered while smiling, nodding, waving. "I can say pretty much whatever I want as long as I smile sweetly for the cameras and we keep our voices low. But there will be a driver in our limo after we finish this little walk-and-wave gig. You have about one minute."

"Fair enough. I'll make this quick then. I apologize for the awkward moment back in the VIP lounge."

In spite of the lack of listening devices, she appreciated that he kept his comment vague with all the people around. However, she also knew this was about as much privacy as they would get for the next couple of days. "I guess there's no need for me to say, 'What moment?' but really Hank, don't give it a second thought. We're old enough to be past worrying about things like that."

"Do you think so?" He cocked a brow. "You don't look too old to me."

And never too old to appreciate what sounded to her ears to be a most sincere compliment. The butterflies in her stomach swirled faster than the snowflakes.

Her publicity smile still in place as she waved and looked ahead, she whispered out of the corner of her mouth, "Lordy, Hank, I'm a forty-nine-year-old mother of four boys."

"And still hot as hell. You always have been."

His words actually sent her stumbling a step on her heels before she regained her balance by gripping his sturdy arm—and making a quick check to be sure no one had overheard that bit of blunt flattery.

Seemed they were in the clear, and she wished she could have credited her slip to an icy patch, except that each footstep hit a swath of red carpet laid expressly for her visit. "Well thank you very much... General." She also couldn't bring herself to leave him out there hanging. "The years have been more than good to you. I was a little afraid I had embarrassed myself back there, too."

His "public smile" relaxed into something more real for a moment. "So basically, you're saying it's okay that we both felt something in the airport lounge?"

"I'm saying we are both normal human beings."

Her waving hand paused for a moment to glide possessively over the crèche. It had been her idea to give away the item to the church in the region where her husband's great-grandmother had been born. Her right. Nothing politically incorrect about it, but everything politically savvy.

So why was her heart aching so over letting go of a piece of artwork she hadn't even set up for the last three years? She told herself maybe she was the only one obsessing about the crèche to avoid thinking overmuch about the more pressing matter of these unexpected feelings for Hank.

"We're also friends, Ginger, and I've learned friendship is rare, unlike…."

Sex?

She didn't know about him, but sex was more than rare for her. It was nonexistent these days. Still, she couldn't miss the depth of what he'd said about friendships being rare, something to treasure.

Their limo loomed a few more steps ahead, the crowds behind them now, the only other observers and press across the lot, roped off.

She stopped, staring up into his golden-brown eyes while waiting for the limo door to be opened. "How have you stayed single this long? You are something special, Hank Renshaw."

Even as she heard the vehicle door click open, she couldn't pull her gaze away from his. She shivered and hugged her wool overcoat closer to her. The weight of the velvet bag on her arm pinched at her skin, the wind swaying the purse back and forth.

Deep in his eyes she saw so much, not just the

shared memory from the airport lounge, but from those years of friendship. Swirling at the center she found times they'd comforted each other—which made her remember the near-crippling agony of losing Benjamin.

Eventually she'd made her way past the pain into a vision of a future full of her children, grandchildren and a career on the national scene full enough to keep her busy for life. It had felt like enough.

Except at the moment she was too aware of the feel of red satin against her skin.

Heaven help her, Hank was reaching toward her. Could he be as caught in this moment as she was? Now wouldn't a single inappropriate touch between the two of them eclipse all other morning feature photos?

She started to caution him when she realized he wasn't reaching to stroke her arm, but to grip her elbow. His mouth opened.

"Ginger. Down," he shouted, just as a bullet split a hole in the red carpet an inch from her high heels.

Chapter 2

Hank flattened Ginger down to the red carpet, shielding her with his body as he weighed his options for the best place for her safety. Bullets came at them from both sides. Security personnel made attempts to rush toward her, but bullets held them off.

Downed two. Holy hell.

Handheld radios squawked as a local cop pointed out a target in a black suit. A man with a sputtering gun keeping them from the airport.

A longer rifle glimmered in the distance from the patch of icy trees. Hank shouted a warning as another hail of gunfire exploded. Good guys and bad guys— all wearing black suits—blended until he didn't know who to trust. No way even of determining who was from what country.

Shielding Ginger, he pivoted left and right, ascertaining one thing for certain. The limo chauffeur narrowed his eyes in their direction.

Hank had a split second to decide whether to put Ginger's life in that man's hands. Hank's training, his instincts all shouted, trust no one.

He went into battle mode. Over thirty years of training kicked into high gear with one objective. Keep Ginger alive.

His arm hooked around her, he pressed her to his side as he ran. He protected her as best he could, shifting his back to whichever way it seemed the barrage of bullets raged worst.

He needed cover. Certainly. More than that he needed to get the hell away. He scanned the field, a mass of mayhem now with the crowds of shrieking observers running for cover behind trees or distant houses.

He missed the good old days when he'd driven himself from point A to point B. The limo was a no-go for transportation even if he could trust—or take out—the chauffeur. The vehicle was too unwieldy and identifiable.

Hank ducked by a tree with Ginger against him as a fresh hail of bullets spat from the airport door. Thank God she wasn't a squealer. She kept her head and her silence. Although she couldn't keep up, thanks to those ridiculous high heels that made her legs dream material.

"Look. There." She pointed to another man dressed in a suit. Appeared to be secret service, but damned if he wasn't pointing his gun in their direction.

His brain raced until the obvious hit him. They couldn't go *inside* the limo, but the back end of the limo would make a fine place to crouch while planning.

Arm around her waist, Hank hefted her off her feet and sprinted back, closer to their original position. Bullets pocked the ground by his polished uniform shoes. Damn it all, he wished he had his flight suit and combat boots rather than this monkey suit with medals clanking and shoes pinching.

Finally, he eased Ginger to the ground. Luckily, the vehicle's engine was off—shot out from bullets perhaps?—so no worries about being run over.

She wrapped her arms around the boxed crèche, her black wool coat trailing in the snow behind her. "What the hell is going on?"

"I don't know, but I'm not sticking around to chat with the guys shooting at us." He slid his hand inside his overcoat and pulled out his 9 mm. "Can't tell the good guys from the bad guys."

He had a gun—of course he did, given the woman he'd been tasked to escort. Right now it was tough to figure out who to shoot. He could just as easily take out one of their own, but by the same token he couldn't bring himself to trust a single person here at the moment. Bottom line, the best course still seemed to be trust no one for the moment, leave and recoup.

Now he had to figure out how to get out surreptitiously—with a hot woman in a red suit who just happened to be the high-profile U.S. Senator from South Carolina.

"Hank?"

"Thinking." He gave her waist a reassuring squeeze. "Hang in there."

"Hank—"

"Damn it, Ginger—"

"Hank!" She thumped his chest and pointed.

Tucked twenty feet or so away under an icicle-laden tree sat a silver Mercedes, engine humming, driver slumped over the steering wheel.

A getaway car.

He smiled.

She winked. "Ready?"

"Set," he growled.

"Go!" Her purse clutched to her chest, she leapt to her feet and ran like hell in those heels he could have sworn would keep her back.

Well, damn. So much for carrying her this time. He bolted after her, his coattails flapping in the wind. He focused on creating a boundary with his body between her and anyone who might target her. Seconds later, they reached the Mercedes. Hank gripped the dead man by the collar and pulled him from the car.

He took a precious extra five seconds to relieve the dead guy of all his weapons before climbing behind the wheel—to find Ginger already buckled in beside him with her black velvet bag containing the family crèche resting on her lap. Her seat was reclined enough to keep her head out of the way of incoming fire.

"Let's blow this pop stand." He stretched his arm along the back of her seat and looked behind them, reversing the vehicle before pulling forward onto the road. Away from the firefight.

God, it felt like an hour since he'd stepped out of that little airport, but the whole ordeal had probably lasted all of ninety seconds. He'd experienced that same bizarre time-warp sensation countless times before in battle.

Now he just had to figure out a safe place to relocate in a foreign country with a U.S. Senator in tow at a time when people had decided to start shooting at her for no apparent reason.

Merry flipping Christmas.

"Buckle up." Ginger couldn't hold back the order as she gripped the dash of the Mercedes they'd just stolen from the dead agent.

"Yeah. In a second." Hank slammed the car into Reverse again as they reached a road block of tractors.

"Now. Buckle it." She put on her best mother voice that had actually stood her in good stead at the bargaining table when working to eliminate pork from legislation. "You're no good to me if you catapult through the windshield in a car chase."

"Uh-huh." He rammed the Mercedes into Drive and nailed the gas pedal, whipping the steering wheel around to dodge the limo that had suddenly taken an interest in them again. Apparently the engine hadn't been dead after all.

"I hear you, Ginger. As soon as I get a hand free. Duck."

A bullet nailed the vehicle. The car rattled on impact. The reverberation shuddered up through her toes. Echoed through memories in her mind. She would never forget the unmistakable sound of tearing metal when she'd lost her husband in that awful car crash on an icy road.

She also couldn't help but think of Hank in battle. How often had Hank heard antiaircraft fire hit his plane? Had it sounded the same? Life was too fragile.

Her heart pounded. She hit the deck as ordered. That didn't mean, however, that she would forget about Hank's safety. If he wouldn't take care of himself, she would do it for him.

Ginger tucked her head low and reached over his lap. He thought he was invincible. She knew better. Images of her dead husband's lifeless body in the wreckage of their family car still haunted her dreams at vulnerable moments. Like now. Here she was again, in a vehicle, driving too fast beside a man who was an important part of her life.

The Mercedes engine roared a reminder of their need to put space between themselves and the current crisis. She could hear the limo behind them. The squeal of brakes. Feel the swish of tires on slushy roads as rubber worked to gain traction.

The luxury sedan lurched forward as if rammed from behind. Hank braced himself. She bit back a scream that reverberated in her mind anyway.

Stop thinking. Take care of Hank's seat belt while he worked his racetrack magic over the streets along the Bavarian border. She stretched her arm, fingers wiggling until she finally…felt… the fabric of his seat belt. Victory. She tucked the shoulder harness under his arm—not optimal, but he wouldn't take his hands off the wheel—and yanked the lap belt in place with a satisfactory *click*.

Relief shimmered through her. He really should know better. He wouldn't climb in a plane without going through a checklist. A rogue thought ticked at her brain like a frosty bracing breath.

He'd been more concerned about her safety than his own. She shivered with her exhale, her breath caressing the rough fabric of his open overcoat.

His coat?

Oh my. What a time to realize she lay with her cheek pressed against his thigh. The heat of him warmed her face chilled by winter and fear. Then her face flamed from more than the feel of him.

Did he notice their suggestive position? She couldn't decide whether she should be more embarrassed if he did or if he *didn't*. She started to shift.

The car jerked left. The brakes shrieked. Hank palmed her back. "Don't move."

She hugged his waist for balance and tried not to envision what was happening outside. The best thing she could do for him was stay calm. He didn't need some screaming, clingy liability distracting him.

Time passed in a blur of growling engines, honking horns, screeching brakes. Finally—she had no idea how much later—the car jerked to a stop. Only then did Ginger realize she'd squeezed her eyes closed during the breakneck chase. Now that the danger seemed to have passed for the moment, her senses went on hyperaware. Her arms were wrapped around the hard muscle of Hank's waist. The fresh smell of his soap mixed with an arousing hint of tangy sweat, no doubt from the run, the adrenaline.

His hand moved along the small of her back. "Ginger? Are you all right?"

"Just catching my breath." She considered herself a strong woman, but she really wasn't ready to open her eyes or sit up just yet. "Do we need to run again?"

"No. I think we've ditched everyone for now."

"Okay." She nodded her head against the coarse fabric of his pants leg.

This had to be the strangest conversation of her life, lying with her head in her friend General Hank Renshaw's lap. She attributed some of it to the flash-back of losing her husband, something she expected she would never fully get over.

Of course it wasn't every day people shot at her.

They'd also shot at Hank, this amazing man who'd stood by her for years, and she owed it to him to be strong because their hides weren't out of the sling yet. Digging deep, she smoothed her frayed nerves and opened her eyes. Only to blink, once, twice, and still find the overwhelming evidence clearly in front of her in Hank's lap. She wasn't alone in becoming aware of feelings other than friendship.

Hank was very impressively affected by their physically compromising position.

Well damn. Here he was, fifty-five years old, and he felt about fifteen around this woman. There wasn't much he could do about this second awkward-as-hell moment as he sat with a sexy lady parked in a car in the deserted woods. Not much he could do…

Except laugh.

He gripped Ginger by the waist and plopped her upright before he did something foolish—like act on the attraction aching through him. "Ginger, I've already told you once today that you're hot. Doesn't mean I respect you any less. We can talk about it more later if you're of a mind to, but right now," he paused and pulled out his cell phone, "we need to find someone we can trust."

"All right." She blinked fast, chewing on her bottom lip, which made him think of that moment her hands had lingered on his shoulders. "And thank you. For the 'hot' comment."

"You're welcome."

She frowned. "Where are we?"

"Near a place I know." He'd had a good dinner here just up this mountain road. "I've been to Germany more times than I can count and made some trips up this way over the Bavarian border. This was all I could pull out of my memory when those guys were chasing us."

"I think it's extraordinary you could remember anything about the area given everywhere you've traveled."

"Piloting, travel, navigation—it's what I do for a living. Or rather what I did before these stars on my shoulders pulled me out of the cockpit and sent me off to deal with mostly political BS."

It had been a lot easier in the days when he'd only had to worry about his own butt on the line. He and his crew, out on a mission. Not a civilian to protect.

Tonight, the stakes were high with Ginger's life in danger for some reason he'd yet to determine.

He didn't have much in his arsenal—a Mercedes, a 9 mm, and the two weapons he'd scooped off the dead guy. Along with his own cell phone and his BlackBerry. And of course his standard stash of currency and an alternative ID he carried with him when he traveled overseas.

"Hey, Ginger, before I start driving again and risk stopping somewhere for gas, you need to take off your shirt."

"Excuse me?"

"Your shirt. Or suit coat or whatever you call it. I'm not up on women's fashion. We have to get rid of that listening device in case someone has activated it. I want to be careful who I speak to."

"Yes, right. I should have thought of that myself." She shrugged out of her large overcoat, then worked her fingers down the gold buttons on the red suit coat, inch by inch revealing the satin camisole again.

He might not be up on women's clothing, but somehow the names for women's lingerie stayed in his mind just fine.

Hank swallowed hard.

He'd noticed her looks before, but never had them gut-slam him like this. That, combined with his deep respect for her and a long-standing friendship, made for a heady combination. Out of respect—and a need to keep his sanity—he looked away at the snowy landscape of pine trees and bare limbs.

Didn't help. His eyes saw tall trees laden with pillows of snow, but his mind filled in the blanks of the rustling going on beside him. Ginger sliding her hand down the front of her camisole as she worked free the listening device.

The world had gone crazy today.

She extended her hand, thin wires wadded up. He took the listening device from her and crushed the mechanism in his fist.

Once satisfied it had been completely destroyed, he nodded. "All right. Time to start making some calls." His phone had the best encryption available. Still, he would keep the conversations short and move locations. "Hopefully this is just a single incident and we can head back in for a late supper."

He offered up his best consoling smile.

"That sounds lovely." She reached under the front seat and came back up with the velvet bag.

Phone gripped in his palm, he hesitated in mid-dial. "You managed to hold on to that through the whole shootout?"

"I must have done it through instinct. I don't remember thinking about it, really. But I'm certainly not leaving a priceless heirloom behind now."

Staring at the steely woman beside him, Hank figured she took the word *priceless* to a new level, a thought more dangerous than any threats lurking behind the icicle-laden landscape. He wouldn't risk anything happening to Ginger tonight, but he couldn't deny his own peace of mind would seriously be at risk if they remained isolated together much longer. He'd only just barely willed away his physical attraction before the shock of having her life in danger, followed by the jolt of awareness over having her sweet curves up close to his body while he was hepped up on adrenaline, took hold.

He definitely needed to get his head back in the game—because it was his job and because he couldn't risk anything happening to the woman next to him.

Hank clutched his cell phone and brought his mind back to the important task at hand. Time to start making calls and hope they netted results. Otherwise he and Ginger would be stuck making use of the Bavarian hospitality undercover.

Chapter 3

Ginger eyed the potato soup in front of her—the price-wise special on the tavern menu—and tried to force herself to eat.

Hank's three calls from their wooded haven had been fruitless so far. None of the people had responded appropriately to his code word, so he couldn't risk giving away their locale.

At least they didn't have to worry about the calls themselves. She knew his phone was encrypted well enough that he should be able to make quick, untraceable calls. With his job, he had *the* best technology available.

Still, making contact involved some level of risk, no

matter how fabulous the equipment. So he didn't want to call too often, which left them in the back corner of a smoky old tavern recharging and regrouping.

In spite of the roaring fire in the garland-strewn hearth, she kept her overcoat on to mask her bright-red suit. She didn't expect people to recognize her, but she didn't want to stand out. Hank had done the same with his coat, keeping it on, as certainly his American uniform with all its medals and stars would draw dangerous attention.

Christmas music from an accordion combated the television and slapdancers to make conversation anonymous, but he'd stayed silent while he ate his bratwurst and potatoes. Was he thinking? Moody? Or just plain hungry?

Ginger glanced around the smoky bar as best she could, taking in the back exit, the bathrooms, the bartender and a couple of patrons at the counter staring up at the television. She wanted to scout out the whole place, but Hank had taken the best seat for viewing. No matter where they went, he always kept his back to the wall. He said it made him feel less vulnerable.

She understood the feeling as well. She didn't much like having her back to this room full of diners when somebody could come through the door, guns blazing, at any second. So why hadn't she simply sat beside him in the booth rather than plopping in the seat across from him with her own back so very exposed, dependent on another for protection?

Because Hank had stand-back vibes right now.

Ginger swallowed a bite of her roll—more like a ball of lead. To hell with this silence. She would force him to talk. They were equal partners in this. "What do you make of the callers not responding to your duress word?"

"Seems less likely that we're dealing with a lone individual out to make an assassination attempt." He filled his mouth with more food.

"A conspiracy?" She prodded, even though the grouch would have to chew for quite a while before he could answer.

"Possibly."

"And?"

Sighing, he set down his fork. "We just don't know the scale or the supporting faction. There were the threats made."

"There are always threats made." She leaned forward on her elbows, her blood chugging through her veins. She might not be able to shoot back at those people out there who'd taken potshots at her, but at least in brainstorming, using her mind, she felt like she was doing something. "It doesn't matter how popular or unpopular a public official is, there will be threats from inside and outside the country."

"You can be sure there are plenty of people working all those angles." He picked up his fork and began attacking his meal again.

Great heavens, he *was* in a mood. She'd never

seen this side of him before. He was as detached as any secret service agent.

Ginger gave up trying to start a conversation and shifted her attention to the television. At least the German sitcom would give her a chance to brush up on her local language skills.

Then the news break came through…

"Hank—" she tugged on his sleeve as the television report translated in her mind "—the news is stating an attempt was made on my life, but that I'm safely back in the care of my consulate. No one even knows I'm gone."

"That's good." He nodded, a hint of a smile showing for the first time since they'd left the airport. "At least the average guy in the next booth won't be looking for us."

Only law-enforcement agencies—and whoever had started shooting at them in the first place if he had connections on the inside. "I really hoped up to now that this was a fluke attempt by one person and we'd get the all clear to come in."

The reality of it hit her. They were truly stuck out here. Alone. Not only was her life at risk, but she'd put Hank in danger, too. That more than anything struck her in the gut, stinging her eyes with tears.

What the hell? She never cried anymore. She knew better because she never knew when cameras might be trained on her. Except, maybe that was the point. For the first time since her husband had raised his right hand and become a senator, since she'd assumed his seat after his death, since she'd won reelection on her own merit—for the first time since then, there was no threat of cameras.

A tear leaked free. "Do you think officials have told my children and yours? I hate to think of how afraid they'll be. They've already lost one parent too early—"

Hank's bodyguard facade slid away and her pal reappeared with a handkerchief in hand. He reached across to swipe the cloth over her cheek. "Hey, hey, now. Nothing's going to happen to you on my watch. Besides, if your boys have been told what's going on, they've also been told you're with me. They know full well I won't let anyone hurt you."

She clutched his hand as she had done hundreds of times in the past. Except today the sensation of his skin on hers felt different against her heightened nerve endings. She almost tugged her hand back but found she really didn't want to. "What do we do next?"

A double-meaning question if ever she'd heard one. Which way would he choose to answer?

Hank glanced at their clasped hands now resting on the table and then at the cell phone. His gaze lingered longer on the phone, his chest heaving with a sigh. "We're on our own until the director of the CIA gets back to me or I can figure out a way to get us to a safe house I know."

A safe house? "How far away is this place?"

"If the weather is kind, we'll be there by morning." He squeezed her fingers. "We're going to be fine, Ginger."

She nodded, soaking up the comfort of his broad hand clasped in hers. She couldn't help but be aware, though, of how in the past he would have given her a comforting hug rather than keep his distance. However, things had changed for them in a silly instant when he'd seen her wearing her favorite red camisole.

"I'm sorry to have pulled you into this mess, but lordy, Hank, I can't help but be glad it's you here with me rather than one of those babies fresh out of secret service training."

"Thanks, but I wish we had a couple of those secret service babies around to watch our backs."

"Fair enough." She couldn't help but think of their battered car outside. "How do you plan to take care of transportation?"

"It's dark enough that the couple of bullets the Mercedes took shouldn't be visible. I'll slap some sludge up over the marks on the back bumper. For good measure, I'm going to swap out our license plate with someone else's in the lot in case someone runs the plates."

"Do you think it has a tracking device?"

He shook his head. "The guy driving it was more of a rent-a-cop variety and the car is older. It's as safe as we're going to get. Stealing another car is risky. Someone might catch us. Even if they don't, there's also the risk of having them report it missing, which gives away the fact we came through here."

"Okay, I can see that."

"Lucky for us, Mercedes are a dime a dozen in this area, which offers a certain anonymity. That should buy us enough time to get where we need to be."

Get there by morning? "It's going to be a long night."

"Then we'd better eat up." He attacked the last bite of bratwurst in front of him.

She shoveled a couple more spoonfuls of soup in her mouth and forced herself to swallow. She reached for her roll just as Hank stared past her, frowning. Her jangled nerves jarred back to life. She followed the direction of his gaze. A burly man leaned over the bar to speak with the guy on duty. The bartender nodded, kept nodding, and Ginger could almost foresee his arm slowly rising, pointing…

Directly at them.

Her heart picking up speed, she shot out of her chair as Hank threw money on the table. He slung his arm around her.

She arched up on her toes to look back. "Duck your head. You're too tall. He'll see you in the crowd."

Hank hunched, pushing his way through the throng, the bar full to the gills with holiday revelers. Ginger crossed her fingers the back door didn't have some kind of alarm because Hank had pointed them in that direction and there would be no time for changing course.

They pushed past a couple on the fringes of the dance floor and made it to the bathrooms by the exit. She exhaled her relief. The door seemed to be nothing more than a simple wooden variety.

Hank twisted the knob and—crap—an alarm blared.

He didn't even have to say *run* this time. She began to sprint only to have him scoop her up again. She really needed to invest in some more practical shoes before this night was over.

Snow hammered down from the sky—a blessing and a curse. A few steps into the storm and already she couldn't see the tavern behind them, which meant their pal couldn't see them either. Only the faint light of the tavern sign managed to flicker through the hammering downpour of snow. Hopefully, their tracks would fill quickly as well.

Hank tossed her in the car before scrambling half over the hood to take the driver's seat. The Mercedes fired right up and dodged around two incoming cars that might have slowed down their pursuer. They were safe for a little longer. But in the bad-news department...

"Hank, I don't think the weather is going to cooperate with your timetable to reach the safe house."

* * *

The weather was definitely not cooperating.

Hank had been scavenging through his memory for a place to take shelter from the snowstorm pounding the Mercedes. The blasting heater couldn't completely combat the frigid nighttime temperatures. Ginger shivered beside him, silent since they'd left the tavern. Luckily, no one seemed to be following them along the winding mountain roads.

However, the storm and remote locale also ended any hope of cell phone communication.

He didn't expect to have reliable connections back any time soon either. Plus, the crummy weather conditions only allowed for a crawling pace. With ice sheeting from the sky, it wouldn't be long before this road closed down, too. While he trusted his driving skills, he'd already watched countless cars spin out and off into ditches, more than once taking other vehicles with them. Very likely someone could hit the Mercedes.

Yet, on the bright side, if the storm kept them from moving, it would also keep whoever had been shooting at them from gaining speed as well. "Are you okay over there?"

Ginger nodded without taking her eyes from the road, a solid wingman from the get-go, calling out reports on conditions and sliding vehicles after translating updates from the radio. But she'd been quiet the last few minutes while the station switched to holiday music. "Just thinking. Wondering how they're going to explain away the cancellation of the big Christmas ceremony at the old chapel while still maintaining I'm not missing."

He swiped at the front windshield, the defroster unable to keep the windows completely clear.

"Have you lost faith in me already? I'll get you there." Of course, first he had to find somewhere for them to stay before the sedan ran out of gas.

He recalled from a trip to the area a chalet where he'd done some sightseeing on his own for a couple of days before returning home. He could have sworn the small hotel was up here, but it had been five or so years ago. The place could have gone out of business or his memory could be faulty.

Not that he'd ever been wrong when it came to navigation. His wife had always sworn she was the one woman married to a man who actually didn't need to stop and ask for directions.

Ginger held that bag of hers in a death grip even though the tires kept firm traction as they wound around a bend through a sleepy mountain village. "I had mixed feelings about this trip from the start, too."

"What do you mean?" He'd learned long ago to trust instincts in the air and on the battlefield. And if nothing else, keeping her talking might relax her.

"I know when I signed on for this job, I gave up a significant amount of my personal time, but I really don't like being away from my family at Christmas."

"Your nerves are just fried. Plus you must be exhausted from all these whistle-stops on the goodwill trek across Europe. You definitely need to talk to your social planner when you get home and have her schedule more downtime. A human being needs to do things like take a drink of water, make an occasional trip to the bathroom."

She grinned, pressed a gloved hand to her lips, a laugh tripping free. "Lord love ya, Hank, I do so enjoy how you can always make me laugh. You're the only person I can relax around other than my kids and yours." She sagged back with a sigh. "I knew I would be apart from my boys for Christmas and thought I'd prepared myself. It's not like I'm always with all of them, but I'm always with at least one of them."

He chuckled low, a little sad. "And it seems like I'm never with any of my children for the holidays, never really have been. We learned to celebrate on whatever days we were together."

"I guess I do remember a few of those sorts of delayed birthdays when Benjamin was on active duty, but he didn't stay in the Air Force long enough for the kids to remember him missing anything significant."

"You're lucky." The memories of those years parted like the windshield wipers slapping away the sheets of snow. "My young'uns remember well. They would say it didn't matter…but I knew better. A live-in nanny wasn't enough, yet it was the best I could do." He studied the road ahead, a narrow path cut by the slim double beams of light. Much like he'd lived his life. "I still wrestle with the guilt over not having gotten out of the military and taken some nine-to-five job."

"Your children grew up into amazing adults, and they all joined the Air Force." Her hand in a black leather glove rested halfway between them on the seat, reaching in comfort, almost there, patting. "I think it must mean they understand that for some people like you, the calling to serve in the armed forces is not something you can deny. It's in your blood."

"They sure each found their own paths. Alicia is one helluva a fighter pilot. That girl never took gruff off of anyone." His daughter with the call sign "Vogue" had an eclectic style to go along with a strut that cut a swath through a very male-dominated world. Damn, but he was proud of her. He was proud of all three of his kids—even if his relationship was easier with some than with others. "Hank Junior and I don't get to talk as much as I would like."

"It's tough flying in your father's plane in the shadow of your father's stars." She leaned her chin on her elbow, staring out the window as they drove past a small pond where a few kids braved the weather to skate by the light of a bonfire.

"I try to stay out of his business." More like his son tried to stay out of his old man's way, which seemed to include not talking all that often.

"But then when it comes to Darcy—"

"Yeah, yeah, she's my baby." His youngest daughter had been kidnapped briefly as a teen in an attempt to get to him. So, of course, his knee-jerk reaction was to check up on her. He tried to rein himself in, and she was a tough cookie who didn't hesitate to tell him when to back off.

He couldn't stop a deep smile from digging into his face. He'd never admitted it to any of them, but Darcy had always been the one who reminded him most of himself. Actually Jessica had pointed out the similarity for the first time.

Why did he keep thinking of his dead wife today? It wasn't that he'd forgotten about her. But as the years went by, he found he could make it through days, then weeks without thinking of her. She would always be a part of his past and a part of him, but his life had gone on.

A week ago, he simply would have turned to Ginger and asked her something about Benjamin, worked the conversation around to how she dealt with it all. Ginger had always been someone he could talk to.

Just ask her, damn it.

Except suddenly the snow parted in a swirl and his chalet appeared, a holiday fresco painted on the outside. The gabled inn was small and snow-covered and welcome as hell.

Ginger shifted in the leather seat next to him, her exhale rattling along with the engine shutting off. "Not exactly how I planned to spend my Christmas week."

He eyed the chalet where he would be sharing a room with his best friend, his *hot* best friend.

"Don't give up on Christmas yet. With luck we'll only have to hide for one night."

This big fluffy robe sure didn't hide as much as she'd like.

Ginger stood in the bathroom doorway, gripping the tie around her waist. It certainly was a long sprint from here to the sleigh bed where she could dive under the plump comforter to wait for her underwear to dry. Oh, but the bed looked inviting and warm where she could sleep with the sound of the fire snapping, the smell of the evergreen garland decorations reminding her of home as she drifted off…

Except Hank sat on the edge of the bed. All six foot three inches of him taking up most of the mattress, his BlackBerry held in his hands as he typed away, oblivious to her.

Wait.

His BlackBerry!

Why hadn't she noticed that before? Good Lord, the man was never without the thing. She'd been so focused on the cell phone, she'd never considered what he could do with e-mail and the Internet, especially with his encryption card. She realized her

BlackBerry had been lost in the scuffle, so she hadn't thought about it again since they'd left the airport.

Rushing past the roaring fire in the stone hearth, she padded on bare feet over to Hank, stopping by his knees. "Do you have a signal? Are you calling someone to come get us?"

"The signal is flickering in and out. I've sent a message that we're still safe. It may or may not have gone through. Beyond that, I'm not hearing anything back. But with things so unsure, I can't risk broadcasting our location to whoever may be on the receiving end of the message."

"We're cut off." Her knees went weak and she dropped to sit on the brocade wingback chair, holding the edges of the robe together while she stretched her legs to wiggle her toes close to the crackling flames. "We should make the most of this time and work on a list of who would want me dead."

"And why." His gaze skipped along her bare calves. "Reasons help."

Sometimes her job really stunk. She tucked her legs underneath her. "You haven't said 'I told you so.'"

"About what?"

She toyed with the robe's tie. "You wanted me to wear a bulletproof vest. If I had, you wouldn't have had to worry about me so much when you were hauling me around that red carpet."

Slowly he looked up from the BlackBerry, his deep dark eyes meeting and holding hers with a power that stilled her. "I would have worried about you anyway, Ginger."

The wind howled. Sleet dinged the windows. And that undeniable attraction hummed along the thread tugging between them. She couldn't ignore the muscular strength of him. The man undoubtedly still worked out. He had the kind of body a woman could curl up against. The sort she knew would keep her warm on cold nights, whether it be about sex or tucking her toes between those solid legs.

She forced herself to swallow. Well, she had to so she could muster up enough moisture to speak. "Thank you." Her mouth dried up again. She looked away from him, to his BlackBerry. "Back to the list."

"Yeah, right." He rubbed his thumbs over the handheld device. "There were the two threats that came in this morning from new terrorist cells that have popped up along the Russian border."

Her cheeks puffed with an exhale. "I remember them from the briefings. You wanted me to bail on today's meeting."

"I wanted more time to gather intel," he gently corrected.

"Let's go over what we do have."

"As I said, both groups are in their infancy, but looking to make a statement. The one we believe sprouted out of Rubistan has yet to lash out." He scratched a hand over his five o'clock shadow. By the bed, the digital clock's glowing little red numbers silently shouted out a reminder of the lateness of the hour—12:13 a.m. "They're still training and posturing."

"Unless today was their opening act." Her eyes slid from the masculine cut of his jaw to his salt-and-pepper hair, trimmed short to military specs. The sprinkles of gray spoke of experience and wisdom. *Strength.* All of those things made him more appealing, especially on a day when she desperately needed a strong protector at her side.

Damn it, she didn't want the heartache of another serious relationship. Why couldn't he do something totally obnoxious? She forced her mind to stay on the task at hand. "And the other group?"

"Has risen from the ashes of the suppressed People's Revolutionary Council in Cantou. They like to dabble in nuclear weaponry. They've already tried to park a bomb in a duffel bag at a German train station. Luckily, the bomb was defused."

"Then they're equal opportunity offenders."

"Apparently so." He cricked his neck from side to side, the white uniform shirt open and displaying a tempting hint of chest. "We have our normal assortment of call-in and write-in threats that come with every event. I wish I had the stack in front of me so I could review—"

"Hank, you know it takes weeks, sometimes months to trace through all of those reports. It would be a duck shoot, hoping we lucked into the right one in time for it to make a difference tonight."

"Instincts count for something when you go duck hunting."

"Do you still think they haven't told the kids about us being missing?"

"Honestly? I don't know."

She stretched her legs in front of her, cracked her toes, then felt the weight of Hank's gaze on her calves again. The logs in the fireplace snapped and popped.

Hank's chest expanded in his uniform shirt. "We'll need to get back on the road the minute the weather breaks."

"Of course."

"You should turn in now and nab as much rest as possible."

Go to bed? Did he intend to get off the mattress before she stretched out? Or was he going to sleep, too?

She couldn't imagine he would give up his watch even though he should snag a couple of hours of shut-eye.

"Uh, I'm going to put my clothes back on first, in case we need to leave quickly." She would simply suffer through damp underwear.

She sprinted for the bathroom and slid back into her clothes, minus the panty hose and high heels. If she'd been alone, she could have slept in the camisole and tap pants… She couldn't resist the grin that thinking of how that would surely make Hank stop in his tracks brought to her face.

"Ginger," his voice called through the wall. "We've got an e-mail."

Chapter 4

Hank jostled the weight of the BlackBerry in his hands as well as the weight of the message in his mind. Could he trust the simple text on a day when shots appeared to have come at him and Ginger from allies? Maybe even from within their own camp?

Ginger sat beside him on the edge of the bed, her fresh-washed hair damp and tousled and tempting right beneath his nose. "Do we trust the all clear to come in?"

"It's not as if we can leave yet with the snow-storm. Once the weather does cooperate, we really don't have a choice but to take this one cautious step at a time."

"Basically, then, the e-mail changes nothing

tonight." Her bare toes curled into the carpet, a sexy temptation, a woman's bare feet and a stretch of naked leg leading into the red skirt.

"Afraid not." He pulled his attention back onto the BlackBerry, a much safer place to look at the moment. "We're still captives of the weather."

She scratched the top of one naked foot with the toes of her other foot. Damn, he was developing a foot fetish.

Hank rose from the edge of the bed, dimming the lights one after the other on his way. "I'll sit over here and see what other information I can milk out of this BlackBerry. You should try to sleep while you can."

"All right. I know it's senseless to insist you need sleep as well."

"I'll rest, catch catnaps. I'm used to pulling long shifts."

Pivoting on her heels, she snorted, mumbling something he could have sworn sounded like "pig-headed men."

He turned away and tried not to listen to the sound of rustling sheets. Good God, how long would it take the woman to find a comfortable spot? A second before his sanity snapped, the sounds quieted.

"Good night, Hank."

Her voice carried across the room with an unmistakable intimacy.

He cleared his throat and forced words free. "G'night, Ginger."

He tapped keys on his BlackBerry and lucked into a solid Internet connection. At least he could do some research on the two terrorist groups that had made the death threats. Was there a significance in the date, this season of unity and hope?

Or was he chasing shadows? He'd been so certain there had been gunshots coming at them from within the protective detail. Everything had happened so quickly, he hadn't recognized each of the faces well enough to know if the shooters were from local forces or their own. He could have sworn at least two of the people who should have been protecting Ginger had been aiming *at* her.

Hank kept tapping through his Internet search, fruitless though it might be, but at least he was *doing* something. Inaction wasn't an option.

Especially once those sheets started rustling again. And again.

He glanced over his shoulder. Ginger thrashed in her sleep. Her feet kicked at the covers as a low moan slipped from her lips.

Hell. No question, this day was the stuff nightmares were made of.

Hank holstered his BlackBerry and shoved to his feet. Four long strides took to him to her side.

"Ginger," he said softly, cupping her shoulder in a careful hand, not wanting to startle her awake. "Ginger, honey, it's okay. You're safe."

Her eyes stayed tightly shut, another moan

slipping free. Apparently the nightmare had deep talons. He knew the sort well from years of combat.

Waking her wouldn't help. She would only remember the horrors all the more vividly. If he could soothe her back into a deep and peaceful sleep, with luck she wouldn't remember the terror come morning.

He hadn't been able to take her to safety yet, but he would give her a serene night's rest. He could help her ease the tight grip of her manicured hands on the sheets. Hank couldn't help but stare at her bare ring finger where Benjamin's family diamond set had once rested. Now she only wore a simple band on her right hand, a ring with her children's birthstones.

Right now he would sacrifice anything to lie there with her. His want warred with his need to continue researching on the Internet, hoping to luck in to some answer.

Ultimately though, as she thrashed from side to side, her comfort was too damn important to him.

Mission set, he stretched slowly beside her, his back against the headboard. He slid an arm along Ginger's shoulders and sure enough, she curled against him with a sigh and stopped kicking. He couldn't ignore how right it felt to hold her there, her soft cheek on his chest, her breath against his neck.

He just wished he knew who she'd reached for in her sleep.

* * *

Sunrise slatted through the small part in the brocade curtains. Ginger sat at the tiny table, surprisingly rested after only five hours sleep, and munched away at an apple from the complimentary basket. She'd also made use of the room's coffeepot, but keeping busy did nothing to ease her nerves.

Reality glared beside her steaming mug in the shape of an ugly black gun Hank had left with her while he took his shower.

She had no doubt that it would be the world's fastest wash up.

Sure enough, the bathroom door opened and Hank's broad shoulders filled the opening. He wore his uniform again, just the shirt and pants, the jacket with its medals and his long overcoat were hanging in the closet.

In the quiet moment before they had to go back out beyond the safe walls, the reality of all they'd been through—all he'd risked for her—crashed down around Ginger again. "Thank you."

"For what?" He scrubbed a towel over his short buzz of hair.

"For putting yourself between me and the gunfire yesterday. For finding this safe place for us. For keeping watch so I could sleep."

"That's my job." He tossed away the towel as easily as he brushed aside her words.

"I know, but you still deserve to be thanked."

She rose, leaving her uneaten breakfast, her nerves too on edge for her to put food in her tumbling stomach anyway.

He retrieved his uniform jacket and overcoat from the closet. "You're scared by what's waiting outside that door."

Perceptive man.

"I'm human and that safe house seems far away. I want to see my children again." She reached to stroke his jaw and couldn't help but linger along his freshly shaven cheek. "And I *don't* want anything to happen to you because you're protecting me."

"I'm good at what I do *and* I'm lucky. Look at how old I am." He winked before finishing buttoning his uniform jacket and donned his overcoat. He extended her long coat for her as well. "I've beaten the odds for years. Now let's go."

He tucked the gun into his pocket, thrust her velvet bag into her hand and reached for the door. The wink and that twinkle in his eyes combined with all the adrenaline of the past twenty-four hours did her in.

That—and the memory of the dent in the pillow next to hers.

Ginger covered his hand with hers on the doorknob. "Hank. Wait. Before we go, there's something I *have* to do first."

She couldn't stop what had been building since the second he'd walked in on her yesterday as she stood in her camisole and she'd seen that flame in his eyes. Since she'd felt an answering heat stoke deep inside her. She saw the question in his gaze. Then the realization. Ginger arched up on her toes and, thank goodness, she hadn't walked out on this branch alone because Hank's mouth met hers.

A first kiss. At her age, she'd thought she was past that teenage tingle of awe shimmering all the way to her toes. Apparently not. Her lips parted under his to admit the bold thrust of his tongue.

Nothing teenage about that. He was a hundred percent mature and experienced *man*.

She looped her arms around his neck and molded herself to him. She'd denied this part of herself for so long it seemed she'd stored a wealth of feelings that were now overflowing. So much so that she feared she might not be able to leave the room for a long time yet, a dangerous proposition for them— literally. They needed to leave.

Ginger forced herself to slide her hands from around his neck down to his chest, drawing her mouth from his kiss, another, then a final nip away. "Okay, we had to get that out of the way or the car ride was going to continue to be really uncomfortable. *Now* we can go."

Her feet not nearly as steady as she would have liked, Ginger scooted past Hank out the door. She heard his muffled curse as he made tracks after her, which made her realize she was even more shaken than she'd realized since she should have let him check the halls first. Well, too late now.

This whole "kiss experiment" had backfired on her. She'd hoped by getting it out of the way, the awkwardness would dissolve. Instead, she'd only made things worse because no way could she have predicted the power of her reaction. She couldn't afford this kind of distraction.

And there was a teeny-tiny part of her that was more than a little scared by the intensity of the moment. She really didn't have the time or emotional energy to sort through all of this now.

Her best bet for today? Pretend this hadn't happened and try to regain their old footing as friends.

So damn close.

They'd almost made it to the safe house. Hank couldn't believe that, after all his worries about gunmen and traitorous moles, they'd been stopped by a simple flat tire and a worn-out spare.

Hank figured the best way to hide today would be to lose themselves in a crowd of shoppers while waiting for the Mercedes's tire to be patched. He'd considered renting another car and hoping they made it to the safe house before the credit card could be traced, but the small village only had one rental place and it had been sold out for the holidays.

And to think the safe house was just a few more miles down the icy road.

His and Ginger's day driving through small towns had been long and tense, but December twenty-third was close to over. He hoped this would be their last stop. No more nights alone together.

He couldn't let himself think about how damn good—how right—it had felt to spend the night with her tucked against him. He hadn't been able to give up the chance even once she'd settled. Instead, he'd simply retrieved his BlackBerry and done his research while holding her.

A bittersweet pleasure he'd thought never to repeat—except then she'd kissed him and now he didn't know what to think, except that they had to get through this day.

The tiny town overflowed with last-minute holiday shoppers clutching bags and the hands of small children. Old-fashioned cast-iron streetlamps adorned with wreaths and ribbons lined the street, ready to flicker to light when the sun went down in the next couple of hours.

With his overcoat covering his uniform, he and Ginger could be locals even—as long as they kept their mouths closed. They actually blended in with the Christmas mayhem as snow flecked from the sky.

He searched the press of bodies around them, suspicious of each bump and jostle of every passerby. He focused on all the details on all the open-air stalls lining the thoroughfare. "Come on. Let's duck out for the next half hour until the tire is ready."

He steered her past a stall selling mugs of warm *gluhwein*—mulled spiced wine. Pushing wide a jingling door, he nudged her inside a tiny shop, away from the crowd.

Ginger stomped the snow off her feet, then glanced around, sighing. "A children's store. This sure brings back memories." She strolled past a display of toy dump trucks, her gaze lingering. "Of course, it's different shopping now since they're all grown up."

"Not that different for me now. I have a grand-daughter, remember?"

"Alicia's daughter." Ginger smiled, the day's worry almost sliding from her features. "Yes, we should find something for her. And does Darcy know the gender of her baby yet?"

His daughter had called just last week with the news. He'd been meaning to tell Ginger, but the grind of this tour had never given them time alone. How strange it had taken an attempt on her life to give them a moment to themselves. "Darcy and Max are expecting a boy."

"So you have one of each to shop for. Definitely fun. Congratulations!"

"Thank you." He'd been thinking of Jessica a lot lately, and how she'd missed out on seeing their grandchildren. Sharing these firsts with Ginger helped ease something inside him.

Then a hint of guilt pinched, surprising him. It had

been a long time since his wife's death, twenty-four years. Must be the holidays making him sentimental, reminding him of holidays past.

Damn it, Ginger was an important person in his life and he owed her better than half his attention. "What are you thinking about?"

She nodded toward the back corner where a Santa in traditional long robes passed out chocolates to children. "Of the history of Santa Claus."

"Saint Nicholas?"

"Yes." She pulled her gaze away with a nostalgic smile, trailing her hand over a wooden train set. "I was thinking of when Jonah heard my Dutch grandmother refer to Santa as Sinter Klaus. He thought she'd said Senator Klaus, because his dad was a senator, the word made sense."

She'd always had a soft spot for her youngest, Jonah. Hank understood well how tough it was to let the youngest leave the nest. His daughter Darcy reminded him often enough that he needed to quit looking over her shoulder. She was a totally qualified and safe aviator.

Seemed like just yesterday he'd been shopping in toy stores for Santa Claus—or Senator Klaus—gifts for his children. "Kids make the holiday, no question. Mine were always very particular about having their own nativity set."

"I didn't know that." She glanced up at him in surprise. "Now that I think back, I don't believe I've seen your house decorated for Christmas after Jessica…"

"Right." He shrugged past that guilt pinch again. "When they went shopping to pick out a crèche, it took them *forever.* Somebody didn't like the sheep in one or the angel in another." He paused by a shelf of toy planes. "I was TDY, and they about drove their nanny crazy searching. Then Alicia figured it out. Why buy a matching set? They each put together an eclectic nativity."

"I like that."

"We were never a family for the coordinated decorated tree. Alicia, my child of the unmatched flair, would have painted all the glass decorations different colors anyway."

"Then she definitely won't want this little dirndl dress for her daughter. How about a polka dot fur jacket?"

"Perfect." He glanced at his watch and out the shop window. "Time to go."

"Of course." Her face sobered as she passed the tiny coat to the cashier to wrap.

He hated that this trip had turned so wrong. "I think it's wonderful that you're donating this crèche when it obviously means so much to you."

"It's just a material possession."

"Just a thing? More like a priceless antique."

"You know I don't like to talk about money." She took the wrapped package from the cashier.

"Spoken like a woman who has cash to burn." He made a more than comfortable living as a general and had invested wisely over the years. But he didn't have *millionaire* attached to his name like the Landis family—nor had he ever aspired to such. He'd always kept his eyes focused on missions rather than mansions.

To be fair, he'd never seen any sign of material-ism from Ginger. "You get tears in your eyes every time you look at that bag. It's obviously priceless for more reasons than the money."

"It's been in the Landis family for fifty years. There are certainly some sentimental memories attached."

"Like the Senator Klaus story."

"Exactly. Matthew and Kyle used to argue every year over where to put the wise men." She strode past the mulled-wine stand back into the bustling crowd. "Matthew is such a traditionalist, like his father. He wanted them right there in the manger. Kyle, however, pointed out that the wise men really didn't show up until two years later, so they should be po-sitioned somewhere outside the manger."

"Careful." He reached to slide his hand between the velvet bag and a trio of children rushing past. Ginger was carrying around a flipping mint, for God's sake. What if one of those kids had been a purse snatcher?

He frowned.

Another possibility hit him. Why had he never considered that Ginger might not be the target, but rather the priceless artifact she'd been carrying? He slid his arm around her shoulders and tucked her closer to his side, making faster tracks through the press of humanity.

Ginger shot a quick, startled glance up at him before continuing, "Every year, my little smart-aleck son would cradle those three porcelain antiques and shake his head, saying, 'Two years, for Pete's sake. That makes them the three wise slackers, if you ask me.'"

"That certainly sounds like Kyle." Hank could envision the boy saying something like that, except Kyle wasn't a boy anymore. He would be turning twenty-seven soon.

Her boys had grown up in a blink. He'd tried to help out when he could, but being on the road so much, he'd barely been there for his own kids. Ginger had done a damn fine job with her sons while launching her own political career.

She was one helluva strong woman. He'd taken her presence in his life for granted for a long time.

Why had he needed a scrap of red satin to open his eyes to the fact that perhaps they had something to offer each other besides friendship? For a supposedly world-class military strategist, he'd certainly missed an obvious answer right in front of his eyes.

He and Ginger could offer each other something more if only he could get them both home safely.

He glanced down the road to see if their car had

been pulled around to the front of the garage yet as the mechanic had promised to do when finished, but no luck.

Damn it, what was taking so long to fix a simple flat? The hair on the back of his neck stood up in that battle-honed sense that something wasn't right.

Screw waiting around for the mechanic to pull his car around front. He was going to light a fire under the man. The risk of staying out in the open was too high. He needed to get Ginger to that safe house now.

And pray the all clear was authentic.

Chapter 5

And just when she'd thought they were in the home stretch.

Damn.

Ginger clutched Hank's tense-as-steel arm and stared at the strange man kneeling beside their car inside the repair shop. His finger probed one of the bullet holes.

That by itself wouldn't have been too much cause for concern. Except the towering man standing beside him peering into the crowds with narrowly slitted eyes sent a shiver down her spine that had nothing to do with the brisk breeze winding a corkscrew path around the shoppers.

Here she'd been worried about something else being wrong with the vehicle. It had held out far past her expectations, surviving a shoot-out, a mad chase and record-breaking storm conditions with only a simple flat tire. Only to be finally detected by…who?

Friends or enemies? "Hank?"

She tugged on his sleeve only to find him already evaluating the situation with keen eyes. "Keep close. Be ready to make fast tracks back into the crowd."

The tall man staring into the shopping masses brushed gazes with her, looking past. Then back.

Holding.

His hand slid inside his long duster, a hint of lethal black gun showing.

Ginger curled her toes in her shoes. "Bolt?"

"Yeah." Hank slid his arm around her waist and tugged her into the anonymous press of merry humanity.

Her heart pounded in sync with their feet, in time with the packages slamming against her legs. "What are we going to do? You said the car-rental place was sold out for the holidays. And you didn't want to draw attention by stealing a car. You said we're close. Are we near enough to walk?"

"No." He kept his arm hooked around her, guiding her through the milling shoppers while making sure they stayed side by side.

"Then what are you doing?"

"Thinking. Hoping."

He hauled her into the anonymity of a cluster of people listening to a quartet of carolers. She wanted to ask more about his "hopeful" plan. Hank always had contingencies lined up for emergencies and this most definitely qualified. She chewed her lip and waited while he stared with searching eyes along the street vendors and stalls to where their pursuer stood by a living crèche, no longer chasing them for the moment, thank heavens.

Hank dipped his face to her ear, his smile brushing her cheek. "Forget worrying about getting caught stealing a car or walking. I've just found our ride."

"You have?" Of course he had. When had Hank ever faltered? Apparently she was the only one who had fears and doubts. "I wouldn't have thought a village this small would have two car-rental places."

"Oh, it doesn't have another *car*-rental place." His smile caressed her cheek, swirling away some doubts but stirring up a lot more questions.

He pointed toward a line of decked-out sleighs.

Ginger tugged the sleigh blanket over her legs to ward off the chill, bells jingling with each step of the two horses' feet through the snowy landscape. Hank had estimated an hour from the village to the safe house by this mode of transportation, which meant they should be arriving in no more than fifteen minutes since he'd paid the driver extra to haul butt.

So far, so good. No sign of their lurking bad guy buddy from the village, and the sleigh ride actually provided a bit of anonymity from the main thoroughfare.

Hank's warm frame radiated heat beside her, close, so close, at times she thought he might even kiss her again. Her heart kicked up pace faster than the cars swishing past on the country road beyond the mask of pine trees.

Their driver seemed to be making good time, happily humming along atonally to whatever he was listening to on the headphones peeking from under his cap.

The snow-laden trees passed in a blur, ancient cottages tucked in the woods at unexpected places, their chimneys puffing smoke into the evening air.

"Here," Hank growled low, pressing something solid into her hand. "You may need this."

She looked down to find a revolver in her hand. "What do you mean? The e-mail said all clear at the safe house. I can understand why you didn't want to risk any stranger coming to pick us up. But what's wrong with us going to a known entity?"

"Contingency plan." He kept his voice low, soft enough not to be overheard by the iPod-addicted driver in the seat in front of them. "If something happens to me."

She swayed, the thought, well, unthinkable. Her fingers closed around the weapon, which also happened to cause them to clench around his hand. "All right."

"Do you know how to use it?"

She welcomed the smile his question brought. "I was shooting targets in the woods with my daddy before I got my driver's license."

He winked and released the gun. The ominous black weapon rested in her lap now instead of her precious crèche, which lay within reach at her booted feet. She covered the gun with the red plaid blanket, then reached to secure her hood around her head while the wind combined with their brisk ride to try and tear off the cover.

Hank flipped up the collar of his coat to protect his ears—simple, but efficient, much like the no-frills man himself. "We don't have much time left to talk, Ginger. Tell me more about the family crèche there. Is that something from your Dutch grandma's side of the family?"

"No, actually, it's a piece from Benjamin's family."

"Do you remember anything more?" He kept one gloved hand in his coat pocket—undoubtedly around *his* gun—while the other stayed around her.

"I seem to recall his father bought it for his mother for Christmas about fifty years ago."

"Anything else?"

"What are you getting at?" She rubbed her hands together under the blanket, then placed them back on the weapon.

"Have you considered that someone may want the crèche instead of you? You said yourself it's a priceless piece of art."

"Oh, wow," she stared at the velvet purse at her feet. "Wow. That makes an obvious kind of sense. Does it have any bearing on what we should do today?"

He brushed at a branch that came close to swatting their heads. Snow still showered down around them, drifts building in the sparsely populated outlying area of the village. "My gut's telling me the safe house really is our best bet."

"Okay."

"That's it? Okay? No questions about whether or not there are moles on the inside waiting there to shoot you since I've given you this gun?" He glanced down at the lump where the blanket covered the weapon.

"If your instincts tell you the odds are better for us to go in, then I trust you."

"In my job."

With those three words and their implication about other aspects, things heated up between them. She tried to think of how to answer him honestly. "You know I keep you with me because you're the one person in my life I can totally trust. Too many times I've found out people only wanted me for access to the Landis fortune or a senatorial ear."

"What if I let you down? I'm not a perfect man."

"You're mighty close." So why couldn't she bring

herself to throw caution to the wind and fling her arms around him for another kiss?

Hank Renshaw was a lot of man to live up to. She'd loved and lost one of those larger-than-life men before and, lordy, they left a huge void behind them.

Her hands starting shaking at just the simple thought.

Simple? Not simple at all. Losing Benjamin had shaken her world to the foundation. Nothing, *nothing* had compared to the agony of that time. Only throwing herself into her job and being a mother had gotten her through.

Any dating she'd done had been totally superficial. She realized full well after that kiss with Hank—after knowing the man—things with him could never be uncomplicated. She stared at the winding street ahead, full of ice and heaven only knew what other roadblocks or hazards.

She wasn't one to take the easy route. A person only had to look at her life to see that.

Hands still trembling inside her leather gloves, she leaned closer to absorb more of his body heat. Sure enough, a jolt of awareness shimmered up her arm, an echo of what she'd felt when they'd kissed.

When his gaze had locked with hers back at the airport lounge.

Things were definitely different. They couldn't resume their old ways. She was scared to her cold toes. She just hoped she could continue to muster the

resolve she'd used in countless international nego-
tiations to carry her through figuring out where this
attraction would lead them.

Hank slid his arms from around her and reached
under the blanket to take one of her hands in his,
holding tight. "Do you need another blanket? You're
shaking pretty hard."

Touching him, she could swear he'd already piled
on a stack of blankets, the comfort of him steaming
through her. "I just want us both to get to that safe
house in one piece."

She squinted to peer through the blur of trees as
best she could, and the roadway behind the traffic
seemed sparse but steady. No suspicious vehicles
slowing to watch them. "Do you think they were on
the lookout back there since we were close to the safe
house? Maybe they were just curious about the car
because of the damage."

"Anything's possible right now." He tapped the
driver on the shoulder. The college-aged student
peeled aside his hat and pulled out one of the ear-
pieces while Hank called out some final directions.
Hank eased back in his seat.

Before she had time to think overlong about what
he'd said, the sleigh whipped onto a tiny rural road
alongside a small row of old townhomes in a con-
verted farmhouse. Window boxes were decorated
with pine boughs and white lights.

Hank leaned over as if to kiss her and whispered

in her ear. "Pretend we've come to visit our European cousins for the holidays."

His mouth sketched across hers before reaching over the seat to pass her the crèche and one of the packages. He paid the driver and helped her from the sleigh, looking for all the world like visiting guests. Except she knew his hand in his pocket gripped a 9 mm as they trudged through the snow toward the corner unit, where a decorated tree glowed in the window.

The door swung open to reveal a dark-haired man wearing corduroy pants and a heavy cardigan. *"Willkommen! Gruss Gott!"* He welcomed them with a thick German accent, puffing away on a pipe. "We've only just started to decorate the tree."

He pulled them both into a hug before lumbering lazily down the walkway to pay off the sleigh driver.

Seemingly in no hurry, their "host" escorted them into the small abode, tugging the door closed behind him. In one of those odd quirks she should have been used to by now, the agent seemed to shed years from his age as he rid himself of his role as quickly as he pulled the pipe from his mouth and tossed it in an ashtray.

The man's smile faded. "General, Senator Landis, thank God you're both safe." He extended his hand, his German accent vanishing to be replaced by a nondescript mid-American-broadcaster-type voice. "I'm Special Agent Rodriquez. Let's step into the briefing room to catch you up to speed on the National Security issues at hand."

Twenty minutes into the brief, Ginger sagged back in one of the kitchen table's wooden chairs. She could hardly believe her ears even as computers with the best world intelligence hummed all around them.

Could things have wrapped themselves up this neatly in the hour while she and Hank had been driving? "And you've questioned them thoroughly?"

Special Agent Rodriquez refilled the three coffee mugs, pulling down a couple more for the pair of agents in the back room. "It's an ongoing investigation, but the People's Revolutionary Council is claiming full responsibility for the attack. The Germans have two leaders of the local cell in custody."

"Then I guess that's it then." Ginger took her refilled mug from the agent, her world still strangely off-kilter despite the thaw in her veins and the safety in her new surroundings. Was it because of what she'd shared with Hank? An unsettling thought that he could hold such sway over her emotions beyond just friendship because of a look, a kiss.

A night in his arms.

Hank tipped his chair back, arms crossed over his chest. "There are more people in their group."

"Very low risk. They're disorganized with their leaders out of commission, and they're not likely to strike in the same place so soon."

Hank rocked his kitchen chair back and forth.

"Fair enough." Still he didn't appear satisfied. "What about our cancelled appearances?"

"We told everyone the stress from the attack had aggravated the senator's ear infection, and she was under doctor's orders to rest. Since you're in safely, we would like to invite those who missed meetings to attend the Christmas Eve dedication service, provided you're still up to making the event, ma'am." The agent reclaimed his seat at the table.

"Absolutely." Ginger couldn't fault how things had been handled. Everything seemed perfect, which meant there was no reason not to continue with the rest of her plans. "The chapel dedication is the most important part of this whole trip. Make whatever security arrangements are necessary."

"Ginger…" Hank's chair thudded to the floor with an ominous thud. A stubborn thud.

"Hank, we can't leave the country on this negative note. It taints all the progress we made in the weeks prior." She stared him down, her mind set in spite of the fact she felt the same unsettling sensation inside of her that she saw echoed in his eyes.

However, she'd been in public service long enough to have had bad feelings come to nothing. She couldn't cancel every event because of a feeling, and this one, passing along the crèche, had somehow become especially important to her for some reason she had yet to pinpoint.

So she locked on Hank's gaze and held until he

blinked first and shifted his attention to the special agent at the table with them.

"I want damn impenetrable security measures at that dedication ceremony, Rodriquez. No screw-ups this time. I want her wrapped in a fortress of protection."

Hank couldn't miss the irony of his wish as he stood at the medieval castle window, looking out over the historic fortress's grounds. He'd wanted Ginger well protected and now he waited with her in an alabaster stone citadel that had withstood centuries of sieges and attacks.

He continued his perusal of the outlying snow-capped land as Ginger bustled behind him, settling into the room, putting away her clothes that had been brought over by the secret service. His room connected through a small sitting area. They'd been assigned the lord and lady of the castle's quarters. He'd been placed close to her for protection, practical, but hell on the willpower since he would be spending the night here with her before tomorrow's Christmas Eve dedication ceremony.

Even with his back turned, he couldn't help but be tuned in to her every movement, his awareness of her pleasure or frustration over the smallest details of the room. Her sigh at the bathroom door meant there wasn't enough elbow room. Her harrumph over the closet stated she didn't approve of the musty scent. A quiet humming noise while she filled the dresser drawers relayed that she liked the flowery smelling pillowy things they'd put in there to scent up the clothes.

God knows how he understood all of that since no one had ever accused him of being Joe Sensitive. But there it was.

And he would damn well lose his mind thinking about how much had shifted between them since he'd held her in his arms last night. Or kissed her this morning.

Better focus on the outside.

His eyes scanned a rocky, icy patch of scarred earth where he suspected there'd once been a moat. An ice-covered lake spread to the right, mountains along the left wrapping behind. Strategically, this had been a well-built home and he couldn't deny the rush as he thought of all those old battles chronicled on the tapestries covering the walls.

How ironic that the castle had survived so much only to have the chapel razed by a fluke of nature fifty years ago. Lightning from a storm had sparked a fire, destroying the chapel along with its contents. The village had been devastated. The fundraising drive in this small town to rebuild the chapel had been a heart-tugging story—just the sort that called to someone like Ginger more than any big-city photo op.

One of the many things he admired about her.

As if drawn against his will, he turned on his boot heels to find her warming her toes by the fire. She toyed with the trailing end of the pine bough attached to the mantel, with red bows and silver glass balls. Her sigh of contentment seared right through him.

Their kiss that morning blazed in his mind and through his body as if it had just happened.

She turned to look at him, the flames from the hearth reflected in her eyes. He kept his gaze firmly off the looming four-poster bed with its poufy comforter across the room and a nice little spread of wine with holiday candies, fruit and nuts beside it.

The firelight brought out her blond hair, showcased the shadows of her every sweet curve, of her hips in formfitting jeans.

Her breasts in that sweater—the woman looked fine in a sweater. He vowed to buy her lots of them, in every color. And yeah, these thoughts were leading him directly down one path.

Hell, he could stare at the moon and there was no ignoring the bed's overpowering presence. In spite of all the danger—perhaps even heightened by the reminder of how easily everything could be taken away—they'd been working toward this moment all day.

His feet carried him to her with a surety he saw in her eyes along with those flames even if the breath she inhaled seemed a little shaky. He stopped in front of her and she dropped her extended legs, her feet resting toes to toes with his.

"So, Ginger, do I take my boots off and stay or not? It's your call."

Her face creased in a smile, her breath seeming a bit steadier this time. "Boots off, flyboy."

She didn't have to tell him twice. He dropped into the wingback chair opposite hers and slid his shoes off, dropping them to the floor, with a *thud* and *thud*, before he extended his hand to her. Without hesitation, Ginger glided up from her chair, sinking into his lap and his arms.

Her mouth met his and confirmed that the attraction, the draw he'd felt when they'd kissed earlier, hadn't been a one-time thing. This was real. Intense. Amazing.

He pulled her closer, tighter, her sighs encouraging as much as the press of her sweet bottom against him. His hands roamed over her back, under the hem of her sweater to find warm skin. He caressed higher, exploring and, hell yeah, enjoying.

Ginger cupped his face in her soft hands and eased away an inch. "Why did we never think to do this before?"

"Oh I thought about it." And much more, but mostly in his dreams. He'd been so set on them as friends.

He'd been an idiot.

She smiled against his mouth. "Why didn't you say something? Do something?"

"The same reason you didn't."

"You're assuming a lot with that statement."

He stared at her silently. Waiting. Yeah, he'd gone out on a limb by insinuating she'd been harboring feelings for longer than just this trip as well, but they'd always been honest with each other. He couldn't see the benefit to either of them in holding back.

The defensive brace of her shoulders relaxed. "You're right, of course. There were moments I wondered what would happen if I made a move on you."

"Except you didn't change things between us either, because we weren't ready," he said with a dawning insightfulness.

"And we are now?"

"I'm not sure about that," he answered as honestly as he could. "At least, readier."

She laughed low, then sobered. "Sex at our age shouldn't be this scary. I thought fears about being emotionally prepared were for teenagers."

"We're wise enough to know this is serious." His hands slowed on her back and he took a moment to absorb the feel of her shoulder blades. A simple touch, but the start of learning every nook and nerve. Baring themselves in that way wasn't something to be taken lightly. "We've both been through a lot."

Her palm fell to rest on his chest, a couple of pine

needles from her fingers catching on his sweater. "We've both lost a lot."

And wasn't that the heart of why he'd held back for so long? The draw between them was intense. Almost too much. Could he—could they both—go through losing something this important again?

All such thoughts needed to take a hike or they would never end up horizontal on that bed together, and he very much wanted to land on that mattress with Ginger. Before he took it further, he needed to hear from her. "What do you want?"

"You."

Because above all he did trust her, he didn't need to ask anything more than that. He took her mouth again, not so gentle a meeting this time. No more questions or hesitation.

He skimmed the sweater over her head to reveal a matching bra. He could well lose his mind thinking about how she'd had all this hot lingerie packed away from the start of their trip across Europe. "I never would have guessed you had a weakness for lacy lingerie. You're so down-to-earth and practical, but then there's the red camisole, now this."

"Practical or not, I'm a woman."

"Believe me, I've never been more aware of that than I am at the moment." He wondered what other luxurious lingerie she'd packed in her suitcase. His pulse hammered hard in his ears as his blood pumped through his veins in double time.

Hank unsnapped her jeans, revealing the top rim of green lace. He growled low, sliding his thumb over the rim of her panties. He grazed his knuckles along the creamy softness of her bare skin, which only served to stir a hunger to feel more of her. All of her.

An urge to have her now warred with the desire to stare at the sexy image of her standing in nothing but her bra and unsnapped pants. Her blond hair was tousled from their kisses, her bare feet with toes still curling and vulnerable, toenails manicured with white tips.

While he stared, she acted. Ginger gripped the bottom of his sweater and bunched the wool in her hands. With a smooth sweep that brought both her arms over her head in a move that had him swallowing hard, she tugged the sweater over his head, momentarily blinding him—damn it.

Then sight returned and he palmed the sweet curve of her bottom to bring her flush against him, skin to skin. It may have been a long time since he'd been with a woman, but he had a solid memory and he knew full well this female felt special.

Someone unique.

He dipped his head for another kiss, his hand plunging into her soft hair again, releasing more of her floral perfume.

Need for her surged through him and he eyed the looming four-poster bed. Making love in the chair could be fun, and certainly worth considering for later. But he had something more intense and thorough in mind for their first time together.

Starting now.

Chapter 6

Oh my, she hadn't expected to find *this* again.

She'd been lucky to enjoy that toe-tingling passion with Benjamin. She'd only expected—maybe—to discover friendship with another man, with the warm comfort of a shoulder to rest her head against.

Even with the sizzle of their morning kiss, the inferno now pulsing through her, the urgency that sent her hands grappling at Hank with frantic need surprised her. Even shocked her. Ginger arched her back, pressing her breasts against his chest.

Her jeans itched against her oversensitized skin. She wanted him to peel them off her. She'd missed being undressed by a man.

More than that, she'd missed undressing a man.

She wanted to see Hank. Her frenzied fingers found their way to his belt buckle. Then, better yet, she uncovered his zipper. He eased her from his lap until they both stood by the roaring fire. He locked his arms low around her, a good thing since her feet weren't all that steady under her as she worked at unfastening his pants.

The raspy glide of his zipper sliding down, down echoed through the room. Hank's pupils widened in response a second before his lids lowered to half-mast and his hands went into action.

His thumbs tucked inside her jeans and began inching them off her body. She was more than happy to help with an extra shimmy and hop as his fingers skimmed over her legs. Ginger kicked the pants free and helped him out of his own until he loomed over her, tanned and toned.

Wow.

Just *wow.*

She'd seen him in swim trunks before and noticed he was a handsome guy, but goodness, had she been wearing blinders? Hank was all man. Hot, solid *man.* She wished she'd been ready for this sooner because she'd certainly been denying herself some major benefits in this friendship.

Ginger pointed one finger and planted it in the middle of his chest, pushing him backward one step at a time. "Bedtime, General."

A smile dented one corner of Hank's wind-weathered face. "Yes, ma'am."

He let her topple him backwards onto the fluffy comforter. One slow step at a time, she advanced, kneeing up onto the bed until she straddled his waist. She brought some experience to this, and she intended to enjoy it to the most...

In case there wasn't a repeat?

The scary notion threatened to chill her at a totally inopportune moment. She focused instead on warming herself with the heat radiating from Hank's muscular body and the crackling fire. She extended her arms in a gesture for him to finish undressing her. As his hands swept up to find the center clasp between her breasts, she couldn't help but think about when he'd touched her there for the first time while fastening the listening device. Her world, her senses, had changed forever in that instant.

Another thought slithered through as she wondered how much more her world would change as they took these touches deeper, to the most intimate of caresses, by making love.

He rolled to his side, stroking her face before reaching off the bed to where his jeans had fallen when he'd kicked them free. "I don't want to break the mood, but I planned, too. During our shopping, I picked up..." His hand came back with a condom.

"Thank goodness you thought of it because yes, there's still the possibility, and heaven forbid I should be an unwed pregnant senator." Yet she'd almost leapt into bed without protection.

Then he robbed her of the ability to think again with the stroke of his hands over bare flesh, his mouth to her breasts. And no way was she missing out on the opportunity to savor every inch of his muscular body, his chest, his legs, the hard hot length of him in her hand.

They weren't inexperienced youths. She knew what she wanted, what she needed and she didn't hesitate to show him. Thank goodness he had the smart sense and a strong enough ego to growl in appreciation.

She was a lucky woman tonight.

He tucked her underneath him and she hooked her arms around his shoulders, gliding a foot along the length of one of his legs. She couldn't stop the purr of pleasure over the warm weight of him settling atop her, the unmistakable pressure of his arousal ready, so near. He smiled, and she held that image in her mind as her eyes drifted closed at the muscle-melting sensation of him sliding inside her.

She wanted to capture each moment of this into her memory but thoughts jumbled with each bold stroke of his body into hers. Somewhere in her scrambled mind, she realized that instincts were taking over. Her legs wrapped around his hips to hold on, tipping her hips for more, wonderful more.

She lost herself in the friction of sweat-slickened skin against skin. Touching. Tasting. Mumbled encouragement and appreciation and moans. Somehow in a distant part of her brain she wondered if their longtime friendship had brought a synchronicity of instinctive knowledge to their coupling, because this went beyond right.

With the building swell inside her, she feared it would end too quickly, yet he seemed to sense her frustration and slowed. Hank rolled to his back, shifting her on top, taking her to the edge again only to stop short. Time and time again, he teased her until she no longer worried about finishing fast at all.

"Enough." She gripped, raked at his back with her nails.

"Not hardly." He nipped at her shoulder.

Still, he tucked her beneath him again and began purposeful thrusts she knew…would carry her…to…

Yes.

Completion.

"Penny for them." Hank popped a candied date into Ginger's mouth, wondering what swirled around in that brilliant mind of hers.

How long had it been since he'd genuinely worried about the inner workings of a female's brain? Not that he didn't care what women thought or felt. But tonight, her emotions mattered on an intensely personal level and, for a man who dealt in a more factual world, reading chick nuances wasn't his strong suit.

"A penny?" Ginger teased a sugar-glazed grape along his mouth. "We're in another country. The currency won't work."

"You're evading." He scooped up a handful of almonds.

"You're perceptive." She snitched a roasted chestnut from his palm and rolled to her back.

He might not be known for being emotionally perceptive, but he could see when a person was avoiding answering. "We've known each other too long to misread."

Her emerald eyes finally slid up to meet his. "What do you see then?"

"You're scared," he said with a sudden surety.

He waited for her to deny it…but she didn't.

A sad smile tipped her kiss-swollen lips. "Seems silly, doesn't it? I'm forty-nine years old, Hank. I'm not some young thing to get all fluttery."

Not young? Maybe. But he couldn't think of a time she'd looked more beautiful to him than now with her hair all tousled around her face, her shoulders bare above the covers, a sexy hint of whisker burn along her neck.

He weighed his words carefully. "When I was a 'young thing' I used to think fifty-five looked old, but now that I'm there, I don't feel old. I believe the heart doesn't have an age."

She blinked fast. "Oh my," she cupped his face, "I never would have guessed you're a closet romantic."

"Shhh." He winced in exaggerated horror. "Don't say it quite so loud. You'll ruin my badass warrior reputation."

"Your secret is safe with me."

He could sense the fear in her as surely as he'd ever felt it radiating off any airman about to head into battle. He couldn't deny some of it stirring in his own gut. He'd been there. Felt the debilitating loss. "I know how you grieved for Benjamin. I was there just like you were there when I lost Jessica. Love like that is only supposed to come around once in a lifetime."

"Soul mates." Surprisingly, the words didn't carry any kind of reverence, more frustration. "It scared me, thinking of all those lonely years, my children so big already since we'd started having them so early." She shook off the faraway look and rejoined him in the present, taking another one of the almonds from his hand. "The offer to take over Benjamin's senatorial seat was a godsend. With all that was going on in Congress, I had something to dig my teeth into."

"You've got fight in you, lady." Total truth, he'd always admired that about her. He wondered why he'd never taken the time to notice all the wonder of Ginger before. "You would have found your way around the grief, but there's no question it's to our country's advantage you channeled that energy into finishing out Benjamin's term."

"When I lost him, I just remember being stunned

at how you survived losing Jessica. I mean, at the time, when she died, I understood the tragedy of it all. Still there's just no way to fully comprehend until it happens to you."

"You had the Congress. I had my small kids. Just about broke my heart watching Alicia trying to mother the two younger ones when she deserved a childhood of her own." He shrugged his shoulders. "I had to keep plugging along."

Her wise eyes filled with indecision. "So what are we doing here?"

She'd turned to him for advice before. Why did now feel different? Still, he pushed ahead to answer as he always did when Ginger looked to him for support. "Acting like damn fool teenagers with our hormones raging out of control."

"Your hormones are out of control around me?"

How could she not know? "Can't you tell? Good Lord, woman. I'm fifty-five years old and we've had sex twice already tonight. There's a good chance you'll get lucky again if you keep wiggling around like that showing me curves that make my hands start itching and another part start—"

She kissed him quiet fast. Then slow. Then again for leisurely fun because she could and had been secretly yearning to for longer than she would admit to him. "I get the picture. And thank you, but I haven't been a teen in a long time, Hank."

Now there was a comment he couldn't let go past.

"You turn me on a helluva lot more than any giggling Barbie doll type."

She swatted at his bare stomach. "You're just trying to get in my pants, and let me tell you, Hank Renshaw, even when I was a teenager, I was never easy to sweet-talk around."

He covered her body with his again, a low growl rumbling his chest. "How about I try a different form of persuasion?"

A knock sounded on the door, jerking his head upward. Ginger tugged on the covers and Hank frowned, readying to call out for whatever room service or maid waited outside to come back later—

The opening door preempted him. What the hell? He'd secured the lock—pissed off already because of the old-fashioned keys. Heads were going to roll in security in about sixty seconds.

But first, he reached for the gun he'd kept on the bedside table for Ginger. Gripping the barrel and blocking Ginger from sight ranked as his number-one priority.

The portal filling with a quartet of men cut short anything else he'd even considered saying as recognition stunned him silent.

The oldest of the crew, apparently the only one not shocked speechless, stepped forward. "Mom?"

"Thank you for a most enjoyable afternoon, Senator Landis."

"Thank *you*, Chancellor. I look forward to the rest

of the visit as well." Ginger gathered her composure as she nodded to the German Chancellor as well as Franz Kohl, the Minister of Arts, and Igor Mashchenko, the Vice-Chancellor from neighboring Kasov. The meeting had been called seconds after she and Hank had tossed out her sons and tossed on some clothes. Which left no time for her or Hank to speak to her sons after the enormously embarrassing encounter.

In the grand hallway outside the dining room, she finished her farewells to the heads of state after their lengthy luncheon. Her eyes lingered on the two special guests as she took a final moment to gather her impressions of them. She thought of Hank's concerns regarding the crèche being the focus of the threats.

Could the Minister of Arts want the crèche for monetary reasons? She studied the ambitious young man, a traditional-looking academic in his layered sweater and jacket with slightly rumpled pants. She could have sworn she caught a hint of paint on his brown leather shoes. His thinning hair, however, had been neatly groomed for the important occasion.

She shifted her attention to their guest from neighboring Kasov, Igor Mashchenko. A grandfatherly figure with a full head of steel-gray hair, he had a regal bearing that inspired confidence. He'd risen to the heights through shrewd investments that had helped finance his rise to power. He definitely didn't need money.

Mashchenko bowed over her hand with an old-world elegance that elicited a low growl from Hank only Ginger would have heard. She lightly elbowed her general in the side before smiling at the visiting dignitary and wishing him farewell until the sunset ceremony.

Now that this final meeting was past, she and Hank had no excuse to avoid what waited in the sitting room back in her quarters.

Walking down the castle corridor with Hank distinctly quiet by her side, she winced to think of the conversation still waiting to happen between her and her boys. She wanted to say it didn't matter what they thought. They were the children and she was the parent.

Except they were adults, and actually their opinions did matter to her. She didn't want dissension in her family. Something special had happened between Hank and her, and she wanted to start things off on the right foot with her boys.

Plus, it was damn embarrassing to be caught *in flagrante delicto,* no matter what her age.

Rounding a corner, she followed the path of sconce lights, updated with bulbs made to resemble candles, as she found her way back to her and Hank's quarters. Strange how, in the past, meetings with the heads of state of other countries had given her less anxiety than the upcoming one with her boys.

Outside the door, Hank gripped her by the arm, stopping her. She blinked, her eyes wide at his public display in touching her in front of the security personnel stationed at the end of the hall.

Given the widening of Hank's pupils, the touch to her arm was only the start of his intent. He leaned closer, his mouth a whisker away from hers. "What happened earlier was amazing and don't you doubt for a minute that, given the chance, I would dive right in for a repeat. Don't let anything that's said in there steal a second of what we had. Got it?"

"Roger that, General."

He nodded, backing away without the kiss. She should have known he wouldn't actually risk her reputation with any outright display. Gracious, his words had bolstered her when she needed it. More of that friendship-knowledge of each other coming into play, she imagined.

Shoulders braced, Ginger swung open the door to find her four sons waiting. Matthew paced. Kyle sprawled. Sebastian tended the fire while Jonah sent text messages on his cell phone.

Her boys. Grown up, but still her babies, each with a wicked little one-sided dimple. She opened her arms. "I can't believe you're all here."

She fell into the familiarity of their boisterous hugs.

Matthew pulled back first, her oldest taking charge as usual, so far keeping his eyes solidly off Hank. "Once we learned of the attempt on your life, nothing would keep us away. Then we got here and found out you were missing…holy hell, Mom."

She should have realized it wouldn't matter whether or not her boys knew she was missing. The shooting incident alone would bring them to her.

Ginger moved deeper into the room with them, toward the sofa. "I thought for sure they would keep this silent for at least a couple of days."

"Mother," Matthew shook his head with an unshakable self-confidence he'd inherited from his father. "I won my seat in the House of Representatives, in case you've forgotten. I have access to information."

And a forceful, no-backing-down determination she suspected he'd made full use of.

"Thank you for worrying, son, but as you can see, my security detail is working overtime." She sank onto the sofa, her boys sitting around her. "I'm in capable hands."

Kyle quirked a brow. "I can certainly see you're in someone's hands."

Leave it to her outspoken Kyle to address the issue first. She could already feel Hank advancing farther into the room with powerful strides. Ginger held up her palm to stall him. She and Hank might not have had time to determine where things were headed between them yet, but without question, they had something special.

She wanted this settled without contention between these important males in her life.

"Excuse me, young man?" Ginger tipped her chin and stared him down. "I'm still your mother."

Sebastian, her middle-child peacemaker, interjected, with both hands raised between them, "You know he's not being disrespectful to you, Ma, or to the General. Kyle simply wants to make sure you're all right in every sense of the word."

Her baby, Jonah, reclined in the wingback, laughing. "Like we have anything to worry about. The General would kick his own ass if he hurt Ma."

A cleared throat reminded them all of Hank hovering behind her. "Damn straight."

Heat crawled up her face.

Good Lord, she wasn't in high school, caught talking about a boy in the lunchroom. Still, these feelings she had felt were just as fresh and new as anything she'd experienced then, combined with the maturity to know how very rare and valuable such emotions were.

Hank put his hands on her shoulders. "However, boys, if you know the first thing about your mother, you understand she can kick my butt all on her own if the need arises. And if you know me at all, you realize the last thing I would ever do is let anybody harm one hair on this lady's head. Are we on the same page here?"

They all nodded, although she noticed that Matthew was a hint slower than the rest to accede.

Hank nodded in return. "Fair enough. Now, as much as I would like to catch up on old times with you four, your mother has some official business to attend to outside." He extended his elbow. "Ginger."

She thought of the gun he always carried. A skitter of unease iced up her spine. They'd caught the confessed perpetrators. Still, security would always be an issue in her job and she hated that she put Hank in harm's way.

She could almost hear him gruffing that he had his own job to perform as a member of the Joint Chiefs of Staff, so get off her haughty high horse.

A smile trembled at her lips as she wondered why she couldn't simply grab hold of this happiness. Oh, how she wished she could spend more time with them since she'd only just darted into the room a minute ago, but she truly did have obligations waiting and she needed to change for her final appearance.

"Mom?" Sebastian's hand came to rest on her shoulder. "Are you all right?"

Ginger gave her grown-up child a quick hug and blinked away the sting of tears. "Of course. I'm just sentimental at the holidays."

But as she and Hank both left to get ready for her final appearance on this Christmas tour, she couldn't stop the fear that happiness would be snatched from her once again.

Hank didn't care that they had an entire flipping courtyard littered with security, even a sniper perched on two parapets. He still had what his youngest daughter would have called the heebie-jeebies.

He tried not to fidget while he sat next to Ginger in the front row of chairs set up in the chapel ruins, but there were just too many people at this sunset dedication ceremony. Dignitaries, locals, media, the military aircrewmen who'd flown him and Ginger around from the start. Not to mention an orchestra, all bundled in jackets under tents erected around the chapel remains.

An earpiece in place, he listened to the security chatter, but it did little to reassure him or stop him from scanning the area. The Christmas decorations of lit trees in every corner, live boughs, bows and floral arrangements were magnificent; still, he couldn't help but think of the personnel who'd tromped through setting up each and every piece.

Most of all, he couldn't help but think of how vulnerable Ginger was, sitting next to him wearing her creamy off-white suit and a matching overcoat. She stood out like a beautiful beacon amid all the formal black and festive red.

A Christmas angel to his Scrooge.

They could *tra-la-la* all they wanted, but he was in more of a *bah-humbug* mood. Something felt off.

Ginger sat perched on the edge of her chair alongside the remains of the stone altar, empty velvet bag in her lap as Franz Kohl made comments about the rarity of the crèche now nestled on the stark stone altar. As if having Ginger here in the open wasn't enough, to up the stakes, his own kids had arrived for the event as well, showing up a mere twenty minutes before showtime.

They all sat in the audience with Ginger's boys, their friends since childhood. Hank eyed them lined along the front row of observers—vulnerable, even if his children were all trained Air Force warriors as well.

His oldest, Alicia, and her husband Josh, who both flew fighter planes, passed their wide-awake baby girl back and forth to quiet her while the Minister of Arts continued his lengthy speech.

Shifting his gaze to his own baby girl, Hank could hardly believe Darcy would be a mother soon. Part of him wanted to launch down there and protect her, but she had her special agent husband sitting next to her on one side and her navigator brother—Hank Junior—on the other. Hank couldn't suppress the twinge of surprise at his son's appearance, since his namesake usually checked out of family stuff, especially if "the old man" was around.

As much as he appreciated their support in showing up, he really wished they were somewhere else tonight. He'd asked them to consider observing from the safety of the castle—but none of them would even consider it.

"Hank," Ginger whispered out of the corner of her mouth, "do you have your BlackBerry with you?"

"Does a rose have thorns?" he answered softly without moving his lips. They'd gotten pretty good at near-silent ventriloquism over the years of sitting in the limelight for hours on end.

She rested a hand on the crook of his arm. "Could you look something up for me without appearing conspicuous?"

"No one will think it's odd if I'm using the thing. What do you need?" He surreptitiously slid his BlackBerry from beneath his jacket and cradled it in his palm, his hand large enough most should never even notice he held it.

"You mentioned not liking the look of Mashchenko."

"That's because he was checking you out." The lech.

"Oh really?"

Hank growled lowly.

"Your instincts are usually right on. Why not run a search on him?"

Hank's eyes shot over to Mashchenko where the older man waited for his turn to speak after Kohl. "Now?"

"Why not now?"

Of course nothing about this weekend had been on anything but a breakneck timetable.

"Okay, sure. We already know he's not from here. He's from the neighboring country of Kasov." Hank tapped through to the green screen for a secure connection with deeper files and typed in Mashchenko's name. The man had a healthy portfolio…but sketchy info on his youth. He'd certainly made something of

himself from very little past, but then many did. Still.
Hank went back to his original gut feeling about the
attack being somehow tied into the crèche. "Where
did you say the crèche came from?"

"An auction in New York City.

"Before that." He eyed the velvet bag in her lap

"The auction house had papers that traced it to a
village outside of Berlin. I thought since it was a
German piece, it would be nice to dedicate it to this
chapel and return it to the same general area."

"Papers can be forged." He gripped her arm and
began hauling her out of her chair. "This ceremony
is officially over—"

A gunshot ricocheted off the stone alter, just
missing the crèche.

"Run!" Hank shouted.

As he ran with Ginger, he searched the crowd to
check on their children. Alicia and her husband
scrambled to safety with the baby, while Darcy's
husband covered his pregnant wife.

Ginger's boys and Hank Junior were all currently
being restrained—looking none too happy about it
as they struggled to get to Ginger, but Hank couldn't
think of that now.

His earpiece blared with a multitude of voices
blasting conflicting instructions and reports. Ginger
sprinted along with him to the side as people scat-
tered. The crowd shrieked and dashed in mayhem,
clearing the chairs and stage. Damn it. He could only
guess where to turn for safety.

The stone altar. He could tuck her into the nook in the back and they would be protected on at least three sides.

Four more pops of gunshots launched another round of shouts. Followed by a bullhorn—and a loudspeaker. "Everyone halt. We have the gunman."

The words repeated in German, again in French and in Russian, until slowly the frantic mass of humanity calmed. A secret service agent inched toward Hank and Ginger. People rose from their crouched positions by chairs and columns. The echo of a mishandled instrument—some kind of string instrument—twanged. A baby whimpered.

Still, Hank kept Ginger tucked behind the stone altar as one of the Christmas trees crashed to the ground. He wasn't risking anything until his gut said to.

The voices in his earpiece slowly quieted to only two or three speaking at once. In the mishmash he did hear the distressing news of a sniper down.

His body curved around Ginger's. Their breaths mingled in the small enclosure. He could feel her heart pounding against his chest, until slowly, his synched-up with hers and he had this sappy romantic image of the two becoming one right here at the altar.

What was the deal with that? An old salty warrior like him thinking something so sentimental? But he couldn't deny what he felt in his gut as much as his heart.

He loved this woman. It didn't take anything away from Jessica, or anything away from Ginger. He was just a freaking lucky man to have such an incredible love twice in a lifetime.

No way did he intend to let her go.

From his hidden position, he forced himself to listen to the settling situation outside. Yes, there was a sniper down. From what he could tell, the other didn't have a clear shot behind the altar if things went bad again, if there was more than one gunman.

Hank used his peripheral vision and found a secret service agent tackling a man with a weapon. Shouts sounded from the pile. Slowly the words became intelligible.

"I'm not taking the fall for this. It's *him*. It's all his doing." The gunman pointed at Igor Mashchenko, the vice-chancellor of Kasov who'd been hitting on Ginger earlier. "He hired me to shoot the crèche and destroy it," he continued to babble, thrashing away. "My people have been trying to take it since she landed on European soil, damn it."

Mashchenko stood between the gunman and Hank, the vice-chancellor only ten feet away. "He is talking crazy nonsense."

"I am not an idiot," the young gunman said, his racing voice beginning to slow, a cunning edge cutting the night air. "I videotaped all of our communications—and our monetary transactions."

Hank didn't like how close Mashchenko stood to

Ginger and began scouting for an alternative place to take cover just as—

An ominous *click, click* sounded.

Mashchenko had trained his weapon on them. "Maybe one of your security men can shoot me, if they are good enough, but I will pop a shot off first." He lifted his head to shout, "Does everyone hear that? I have a weapon strong enough to pierce through the General and kill the lovely senator—that is, if I don't hit her anyway."

Hank held tight, but it didn't matter, damn it, because the bastard already had a gun pointed toward Ginger's head and the sharpshooters weren't an option any longer.

"Why, Mashchenko?" Ginger's voice didn't even shake as she tried to shrug her way free of Hank, but he wasn't budging. "Why are you doing this?"

"You have brought that nativity back out in the open." The older man moved closer, the lethal weapon all the closer. "The crèche would be back where it originally belonged. I tried to simply steal the crèche back, but Senator Landis never let it out of her sight. As time drew near, I've had to resort to desperate measures. Now that it is out there, where people in this part of the world can examine it, I will be ruined."

Back where it belonged. But the precious art collection in the chapel had been destroyed by a fluke fire.

Or not.

Ginger gasped. "You burned down this chapel during a storm—after looting the place to sell the invaluable treasures on the black market."

"You're a smart woman," Mashchenko replied. "I was only sixteen but I had dreams and a plan."

Hank couldn't help but fill in the blanks. Talking would buy time, and damn it, if the guy managed to squeeze off a shot… "The money financed your rise in government."

"Enough talk." He waved his weapon, obviously relying on firepower to overcome what he lacked in strength due to age. "There's no reason why we all can't end this day happy. If I kill you, I'm a marked man for life. I just want out now. I can hide. Come quietly until I can get to my connections."

Fat chance.

Hank decided that age didn't have a thing to do with any of it. He'd never felt more honed than at the moment as years of experience blended with training and a deep-rooted need to protect the woman he loved.

As if sensing his intent, Ginger gripped his clothes tighter; with those snipers out of commission, he couldn't afford to hesitate.

The second he saw that Mashchenko's weapon wavered and was only pointed at him, Hank leapt, not far at all. The weapon discharged. Ginger screamed. Hank couldn't afford to hesitate. He forced himself to focus on the mission.

Take down Mashchenko.

Save Ginger.

Muscles bunched, Hank landed on the older male—a man who obviously worked out. Still, Hank gripped the bastard's gun hand in a relentless grip, banging it against the rocky remains of the floor again and again. Praying the villainous thief wouldn't get another shot off.

The thought of losing Ginger was inconceivable.

Even the notion caused a fresh pulse of adrenaline to surge through him, managing to mask most of the pain in his hand as he battered the villain's arm against the ground. He slammed Mashchenko's wrist against a sharp stone one last time.

The weapon skittered away along the cobblestones.

Hank's fist followed as quickly across the man's jaw, knocking him out a second before the secret service descended, Ginger's sons leading the pack to rush them. A swarm of activity buzzed all around them, but his focus was only on one woman.

Where it belonged.

He pivoted to find Ginger already launching toward him—his feisty Carolina angel—blessedly safe and unharmed. He opened his arms to have her fall against his chest where he now knew she belonged.

For a lifetime.

Three hours later—which felt like a lifetime, so much had happened—Ginger stood with Hank under one of the tents erected for the dedication ceremony. After the shooting, it had been changed into a questioning center for the police to collect data, but most of the crowd and media had cleared away now.

A paramedic was just finishing splinting Hank's two broken fingers from when he'd grappled with Mashchenko to pound the gun from the villain's hand. Her pugnacious general insisted he would go to the hospital in the morning. Tonight, give him some tape and a Tylenol. He just wanted to be with his family—the Renshaws *and* the Landises.

She couldn't stop the warm spread of joy over his words, even if they had been spoken with a grumpy-bear growl.

She hoped the secret service would let their children come over sometime soon. At least no one had been seriously injured. The sharpshooter had been hit in the shoulder and was reported to be doing well in surgery.

The stray bullet from Mashchenko's gun, as he and Hank struggled, had struck one of the aircrew—who'd been with them from the start of this trip—in the arm. A superficial wound, thank God.

The injured sergeant was already being lauded by the press as the hero of the day as he'd helped carry an elderly woman to safety during the fracas.

Ginger sank back in the chilly metal chair and stared up at the moonlit sky, stars shining through clearly as midnight approached for Christmas Eve to pass away into Christmas morning.

While she was so relieved everyone would be all right, still she couldn't help but be sad that she'd missed the chance to donate her crèche as planned. Such a silly thing to regret when she considered the larger implication of what could have happened, but as she sat here next to Hank, she couldn't deny the truth any longer.

Giving away that family nativity, something that had been an integral part of her life with Benjamin from their first Christmas together, had been her way of saying goodbye. Because, finally, she was ready.

Ready to let go. Ready to love again.

Ready to love Hank.

Once his hand had been bandaged, Hank waved away the offer of a hypodermic needle that apparently held something with a little more kick than Tylenol. Her heart pounded faster as she thought of the two of them getting swallowed up by the media again, then their families, then their jobs. It seemed as if there might never be another chance for them to talk.

If nothing else, tonight she'd learned to grasp every moment.

She turned her chair to face his as the medical technician reluctantly stashed her needle back in a supply case and stalked away. Ginger took in the powerful set to Hank's shoulders in his uniform, the slight dampness from snow and his injured hand the only signs he'd almost lost his life trying to save hers.

She refused to let the lump welling in her throat

steal her ability to say the words hammering at her heart. "We probably only have a minute or two before the security folks unleash the kids on us, so I'm going to talk fast because I don't want to wait another second to say a few things that should have been said a long time ago."

"Okay." He settled back into his seat, warding off a circling police officer who obviously wanted a word with him.

Her heart pounding, hopeful, she gasped in a deep breath of the icy night air. "You asked about me being afraid. About my feelings when I lost Benjamin. What happened out here tonight made me remember that there are no guarantees of tomorrow. This is a scary world we live in—whether it's a terrorist, a crook or a fluke of fate."

"Where does that revelation leave us?"

"Oh, Hank, it made me realize I'm an extremely brave woman. Sure I'm scared. Who wouldn't be? But you're more than worth the risk. *We're* worth the risk."

"You're also a very smart woman." He glanced around at the remaining crowd, his gaze landing on their children waiting not so patiently by two local police officers. "I guess the only question left to ask is whether or not you're an impulsive woman?"

"Why do you want to know?"

He took her hands in his uninjured one. "Ginger, you've been my best friend for most of my adult life, and now you're my lover, too. I've always loved

you. Today I learned that I'm also in love with you."
He slid down on one knee. "So how about tonight
you become my wife?"

"Tonight?" She blinked fast, in time with the
cameras of the few media hounds who'd stuck
around to the end already click, click, clicking away.
Apparently their moment wasn't quite as private as
she'd hoped.

But oh my, she had the feeling this was one
moment she wouldn't mind having captured on film.

"The priest who came for the dedication ceremony is still around. Our children are all here." His
smile broadened until it lit his eyes brighter than the
Christmas stars overhead. "And you've never been
more beautiful. I can't think of a more perfect time
or setting." He brought her hands to his mouth for a
kiss. "The only thing I need to know is if you're in
love with me, too."

In love? It was as though her head was spinning
from too much warmed *gluhwein,* her heart overflowing with more emotion than one woman could
process. "As you said, I'm a very smart woman.
Although actually, I find I'm listening to my heart's
IQ right now and it says, absolutely, totally, I am
completely in love with you."

She flung her arms around his neck and to hell
with the cameras. She was seconds away from
becoming Ginger Landis Renshaw anyhow.

The marriage might not be official until they

could get back to the States, but as of this night, Hank would be her husband.

He pulled back with a smile meant only for her before he stepped away to speak to the crowd, starting with her sons. "Boys, do you mind if I marry your mother here, tonight?"

The four brothers stepped free from the applauding police and clapped him on the back with a yes, some laughter—and a definite welcome. The Renshaw offspring and their spouses followed closely behind with smiles and hugs, and the flailing joy of Alicia's baby girl. The priest joined the fold, camera lights kicking back into full-blown blinding mode at a goodwill stop that had turned into a media blitz beyond the journalists' expectations. Definitely a bonus to all who'd braved the cold to stay to the end of this event.

Kyle grinned with that one-sided smile indigenous to all the Landis men. "About damn time. I was starting to wonder if we were going to have to dub you the fourth wise slacker."

Ginger stood in the middle of her growing family, Hank's strong—oh so sexy—muscular arm around her waist, and wondered how she'd gotten this lucky. The tiny crèche sat nestled on the stone altar, not officially dedicated, but home all the same and she realized she didn't have to let go of her past to step forward into the future. Both could be a part of her, blending to make her the woman she wanted to be:

wife, mother, grandmother—senator. Lucky lady all the way around.

She and Hank had taken a while to find each other this way, but he was right. The timing *was* perfect. Stars twinkled overhead as Christmas Eve melded into Christmas Day. Their children gathered around the stone altar where the crèche rested. The priest stood in front, reciting the ceremony in heavily accented English until finally the time came to kiss the bride.

Hank whispered warmly against her lips, "Merry Christmas, my love. You'll never have to worry about me forgetting our anniversary."

"Smart man." Her laughter rang along with local church bells, and then just the bells sang as Hank claimed his kiss.

* * * * *

Don't miss Catherine Mann's next release,
THE EXECUTIVE'S SURPRISE BABY,
on sale in December from Silhouette Desire.
And look for the story of the
injured airman as Catherine's
WINGMEN WARRIORS series continues
next year in Silhouette Romantic Suspense.

SPECIAL EDITION*

LIFE, LOVE AND FAMILY

*These contemporary romances will strike a chord
with you as heroines juggle life
and relationships on their way to true love.*

New York Times *bestselling author*
Linda Lael Miller brings you a
BRAND-NEW contemporary story
featuring her fan-favorite McKettrick family.

Meg McKettrick is surprised to be reunited
with her high school flame, Brad O'Ballivan.
After enjoying a career as a country-and-
western singer, Brad aches for a home and
family…and seeing Meg again makes him
realize he still loves her. But their pride
manages to interfere with love…until an unexpected matchmaker gets involved.

*Turn the page for a sneak preview of
THE McKETTRICK WAY
by Linda Lael Miller.
On sale November 20,
wherever books are sold.*

Brad shoved the truck into gear and drove to the bottom of the hill, where the road forked. Turn left, and he'd be home in five minutes. Turn right, and he was headed for Indian Rock.

He had no damn business going to Indian Rock.

He had nothing to say to Meg McKettrick, and if he never set eyes on the woman again, it would be two weeks too soon.

He turned right.

He couldn't have said why.

He just drove straight to the Dixie Dog Drive-In.

Back in the day, he and Meg used to meet at the Dixie Dog, by tacit agreement, when either of them had been away. It had been some kind of universe thing, purely intuitive.

Passing familiar landmarks, Brad told himself he ought to turn around. The old days were gone. Things had ended badly between him and Meg anyhow, and she wasn't going to be at the Dixie Dog.

He kept driving.

He rounded a bend, and there was the Dixie Dog. Its big neon sign, a giant hot dog, was all lit up and going through its corny sequence—first it was covered in red squiggles of light, meant to suggest ketchup, and then yellow, for mustard.

Brad pulled into one of the slots next to a speaker, rolled down the truck window and ordered.

A girl roller-skated out with the order about five minutes later.

When she wheeled up to the driver's window, smiling, her eyes went wide with recognition, and she dropped the tray with a clatter.

Silently Brad swore. Damn if he hadn't forgotten he was a famous country singer.

The girl, a skinny thing wearing too much eye makeup, immediately started to cry. "I'm sorry!" she sobbed, squatting to gather up the mess.

"It's okay," Brad answered quietly, leaning to look down at her, catching a glimpse of her plastic name tag. "It's okay, Mandy. No harm done."

"I'll get you another dog and a shake right away, Mr. O'Ballivan!"

"Mandy?"

She stared up at him pitifully, sniffling. Thanks to the copious tears, most of the goop on her eyes had slid south. "Yes?"

"When you go back inside, could you not mention seeing me?"

"But you're Brad O'Ballivan!"

"Yeah," he answered, suppressing a sigh. "I know."

She rolled a little closer. "You wouldn't happen to have a picture you could autograph for me, would you?"

"Not with me," Brad answered.

"You could sign this napkin, though," Mandy said. "It's only got a little chocolate on the corner."

Brad took the paper napkin and her order pen, and scrawled his name. Handed both items back through the window.

She turned and whizzed back toward the side entrance to the Dixie Dog.

Brad waited, marveling that he hadn't considered incidents like this one before he'd decided to come back home. In retrospect, it seemed shortsighted, to say the least, but the truth was, he'd expected to be— Brad O'Ballivan.

Presently Mandy skated back out again, and this time she managed to hold on to the tray.

"I didn't tell a soul!" she whispered. "But Heather and Darlene *both* asked me why my mascara was all smeared." Efficiently she hooked the tray onto the bottom edge of the window.

Brad extended payment, but Mandy shook her head.

"The boss said it's on the house, since I dumped your first order on the ground."

He smiled. "Okay, then. Thanks."

Mandy retreated, and Brad was just reaching for the food when a bright red Blazer whipped into the space beside his. The driver's door sprang open, crashing into the metal speaker, and somebody got out in a hurry.

Something quickened inside Brad.

And in the next moment Meg McKettrick was standing practically on his running board, her blue eyes blazing.

Brad grinned. "I guess you're not over me after all," he said.

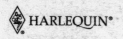

HARLEQUIN®

American ★ Romance®

Kate Merrill had grown up convinced
that the most attractive men were incapable
of ever settling down. Yet the harder she
resisted the superstar photographer
Tyler Nichols, the more persistent the
handsome world traveler became.
So by the time Christmas arrived, there
was only one wish on her holiday list—
that she was wrong!

LOOK FOR

THE CHRISTMAS DATE

BY

Michele Dunaway

**Available December
wherever you buy books**

REQUEST YOUR FREE BOOKS!

2 FREE NOVELS PLUS 2 FREE GIFTS!

Silhouette® Romantic

SUSPENSE

Sparked by Danger, Fueled by Passion!

YES! Please send me 2 FREE Silhouette® Romantic Suspense novels and my 2 FREE gifts. After receiving them, if I don't wish to receive any more books, I can return the shipping statement marked "cancel." If I don't cancel, I will receive 4 brand-new novels every month and be billed just $4.24 per book in the U.S., or $4.99 per book in Canada, plus 25¢ shipping and handling per book plus applicable taxes, if any*. That's a savings of at least 15% off the cover price! I understand that accepting the 2 free books and gifts places me under no obligation to buy anything. I can always return a shipment and cancel at any time. Even if I never buy another book from Silhouette, the two free books and gifts are mine to keep forever.

240 SDN EEX6   340 SDN EEYJ

Name	(PLEASE PRINT)
Address	Apt. #
City	State/Prov.	Zip/Postal Code

Signature (if under 18, a parent or guardian must sign)

Mail to the Silhouette Reader Service™:
IN U.S.A.: P.O. Box 1867, Buffalo, NY 14240-1867
IN CANADA: P.O. Box 609, Fort Erie, Ontario L2A 5X3

Not valid to current Silhouette Intimate Moments subscribers.

Want to try two free books from another line?
Call 1-800-873-8635 or visit www.morefreebooks.com.

* Terms and prices subject to change without notice. NY residents add applicable sales tax. Canadian residents will be charged applicable provincial taxes and GST. This offer is limited to one order per household. All orders subject to approval. Credit or debit balances in a customer's account(s) may be offset by any other outstanding balance owed by or to the customer. Please allow 4 to 6 weeks for delivery.

Your Privacy: Silhouette is committed to protecting your privacy. Our Privacy Policy is available online at www.eHarlequin.com or upon request from the Reader Service. From time to time we make our lists of customers available to reputable firms who may have a product or service of interest to you. If you would prefer we not share your name and address, please check here. ☐

SRS07

Inside ROMANCE

Stay up-to-date on all your romance reading news!

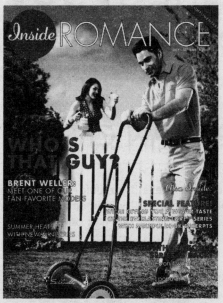

Inside Romance is a FREE quarterly newsletter highlighting our upcoming series releases and promotions.

Visit
www.eHarlequin.com/InsideRomance
to sign up to receive our complimentary newsletter today!

IRN1107

Get ready to meet

THREE WISE WOMEN

with stories by

DONNA BIRDSELL,
LISA CHILDS

and

SUSAN CROSBY.

Don't miss these three unforgettable stories about modern-day women and the love and new lives they find on Christmas.

Look for *Three Wise Women*
Available December wherever you buy books.

Romantic

SUSPENSE

COMING NEXT MONTH

#1491 HER SWORN PROTECTOR—Marie Ferrarella
The Doctors Pulaski

Cardiologist Kady Pulaski is the only witness to a billionaire shipping magnate's murder. Now the former billionaire's bodyguard, Byron Kennedy, must keep Kady alive long enough to testify against the killer. But can he withstand his attraction to the fiery doctor?

#1492 LAZLO'S LAST STAND—Kathleen Creighton
Mission: Impassioned

When a series of violent attacks afflicts the Lazlo Group, security expert Corbett Lazlo asks Lucia Cordez to play his lover to lure the assassins out of hiding. And as the escalating threat forces them to hole up in intimate quarters, their growing feelings for each other could be an even greater danger.

#1493 DEADLY TEMPTATION—Justine Davis
Redstone, Incorporated

Redstone agent Liana Kiley is stunned to discover that the heroic lawman who saved her life years ago is wanted for corruption...and she's determined to investigate the case. Detective Logan Beck is not happy about dragging Liana back into danger, but with a perfect frame closing in around him, he must put his life—and heart—in her hands.

#1494 THE MEDUSA SEDUCTION—Cindy Dees
The Medusa Project

To catch one of the world's most dangerous terrorists, army captain Brian Riley must abduct and transform civilian Sophie Giovanni into a commando. Sophie is the one woman who can identify Brian's target, but with time running out he must choose between his loyalty to his agency and the woman who's stolen his heart.

SRSCNM1107